“I thought you were avoiding me.”

Naomi smiled. “I thought *you* were avoiding *me*.”

They both laughed. It felt good to understand one another.

“I was trying to respect you and give you space,” Gideon said.

“I was trying to keep Miriam from thinking that we liked each other.”

Gideon nodded. “I wondered about that.”

“You thought I didn’t want to spend time with you?”

Gideon raised his hands. “I wasn’t sure.”

Naomi shook her head. “That wasn’t it at all.”

“I see that now.”

They stared at one another without speaking. Gideon could hear his heartbeat pounding in his ears and was certain that he could sense hers.

“Naomi!” Her sister’s voice called out across the farmyard.

They jerked apart.

“You got the feed?” her sister asked from the doorway.

“*Ya!*” Naomi called back.

“I’ll get it,” Gideon said, loudly enough for his voice to carry, then nodded at Naomi.

His hands were soon busy with work, but his mind could only focus on one thing.

What happens now? He did not know the answer to Naomi’s question.

Virginia Wise combines her love of romance, family and Plain living to create uplifting stories set in idyllic Amish communities. Her favorite pastimes include wandering Lancaster County's Amish country and meeting new people who inspire her novels. She also loves meeting the people who read her books and is always eager to hear from them. When she's not working, Virginia enjoys painting, spending time with family and friends, and taking long walks in the woods.

Books by Virginia Wise

Love Inspired

An Amish Christmas Inheritance
The Secret Amish Admirer
Healed by the Amish Nanny
A Home for His Amish Children
The Amish Baby Scandal

Sisters of Stoneybrook Farm

His Amish Christmas Surprise
Falling for the Amish Rival
A Forbidden Amish Suitor

Visit the Author Profile page at LoveInspired.com.

A FORBIDDEN AMISH SUITOR

VIRGINIA WISE

LOVE INSPIRED
INSPIRATIONAL ROMANCE

FSC
www.fsc.org
MIX
Paper | Supporting responsible forestry
FSC® C021394

LOVE INSPIRED®
INSPIRATIONAL ROMANCE

PLEASE RECYCLE
THIS PRODUCT IS RECYCLABLE
Recycling programs for this product may not exist in your area.

ISBN-13: 978-1-335-62161-0

A Forbidden Amish Suitor

For questions and comments about the quality of this book, please contact us at CustomerService@Harlequin.com.

® is a trademark of Harlequin Enterprises ULC.

Love Inspired
22 Adelaide St. West, 41st Floor
Toronto, Ontario M5H 4E3, Canada
www.LoveInspired.com

HarperCollins Publishers
Macken House, 39/40 Mayor Street Upper,
Dublin 1, D01 C9W8, Ireland
www.HarperCollins.com

Printed in Lithuania

God setteth the solitary in families: he bringeth out
those which are bound with chains.

—*Psalm* 68:6

To my very talented niece, Eloise

Chapter One

Naomi Stoltzfus was not sure that she had heard correctly. "You want a stranger to move into Stoneybrook Farm with us?" Naomi did not say what she was really thinking—a strange *man.* Her mind was already spinning with visions of a handsome, mysterious suitor who could sweep her off her feet. The scenario sounded just like the Amish romance novels that she secretly read. Her sisters Miriam, Amanda, and Leah would make fun of her if they knew. They always warned her that she was too much of a romantic for her own good.

"*Vell*, he may be a stranger, but his bishop back in Holmes County vouched for him," Viola Esch said. She peered down her bifocals with an air of annoyance that anyone would question her plan. At ninety-three years old, Viola had spent decades meddling in the affairs of the Bluebird Hills church district. And, more often than not, she somehow got it right.

Bishop Amos took a bite of a gingersnap cookie, nodding his head as he chewed. When he and Viola had unexpectedly appeared at the front door of the Stoltzfus farmhouse a few minutes earlier, Naomi had scrambled to grab a tin of cookies and coffee to pass around. Now, as Viola, Bishop Amos, Naomi's sisters, and her brother, Benjamin, sat in their living room, Naomi forgot to eat. Her mug of coffee grew cold in her hands as she leaned forward, waiting to hear more.

Bishop Amos was a slight man with a sharp nose, rosy cheeks, and wizened expression that gave him the look of a jovial gnome. His big personality made up for his small frame and his eyes lit up as he began to speak. "We don't know Gideon Fisher, but we do know that we can make a difference in his life."

Miriam listened intently and Naomi knew that her oldest sister was sizing up the situation. After their parents died in a car accident with a hired *Englisch* driver a decade ago, Miriam had raised her younger siblings and kept their family business running, growing their goat farm to become the biggest, most prosperous one in Lancaster County. But the pressure had hardened her. She would respond to this situation with logic, not emotion.

Naomi, on the other hand, craved the love and attention she'd lost when their parents died. She jumped at the chance to meet new people—especially potentially handsome male ones. "Tell us more about him," she said.

"He's twenty-two, and is from Holmes County, Ohio," Amos said. "He was orphaned at fourteen, soon after he finished his last year of schooling, and has been on his own ever since."

"We have to take him in," Naomi said.

"He didn't have a foster family?" Miriam asked. "Or siblings?"

Viola shook her head. "He lived with different families while he was teenager, but they didn't take him in as a *sohn*. He was a *gut* worker." After graduating from eighth grade, Amish *youngies* often hired themselves out to families before they got married and settled down.

"He's all alone in the world." Naomi tapped a finger

against the mug in her hands. She was already planning the cake she would bake to welcome him into their home. He needed her. And, she hoped, the feeling would be mutual.

Miriam made a waving motion to quiet Naomi. "What else do you know about him?"

Viola smiled. "He's waiting outside. Why don't you ask him yourself?"

Naomi's eyes flew to the door, even though she knew he wasn't in the house yet. Miriam frowned. Benjamin grinned. Leah and Amanda glanced at one another.

Amos winked at Miriam. "Viola thought it best to bring him here, so he can move in right away. And you know there's no arguing with Viola."

"And don't you forget it." Viola tapped the end of her cane against the worn floorboard for emphasis.

Naomi popped up from the couch. "I'll tell him to *kumme* in!"

"There's just one more thing that you'll need to consider," Amos said. He ran his fingers through his long, white beard.

Naomi hovered in place.

Viola made a motion with her hand as if throwing something away. "It's nothing."

"We'll let them decide," Amos said.

"*Vell*, what is it?" Naomi asked. Anticipation rippled through her.

"He had a little trouble with the law a while back," Viola said. Her expression was firm, daring anyone to question her assessment.

Miriam straightened in her seat. "Viola, we need to know if it's *oll recht* for him to share our home."

"You let John stay here when he was a stranger—and an *Englischer*," Naomi said.

"That's true," Leah said. John had moved in with his new-born baby, Abby, when he was a single dad and needed support. He and Leah had unexpectedly fallen in love and were now happily married.

"John wasn't a criminal," Miriam said. "And he grew up in the Little Creek church district before he left the Amish. Bishop Amos knew him."

"Gideon isn't a criminal." Viola pointed her cane at Miriam. "He just had a little trouble, that's all. We forgive and welcome repentant sinners back, ain't so?"

"*Ya*, but..." Miriam glanced at Amanda.

Viola set the end of her cane back down on the floor. "No *buts* about it."

"Vell..."

"Let's bring him in," Bishop Amos said. "You can decide what to do after you meet him. I'm not telling you to open your home to him, just suggesting."

Viola huffed. "I'm telling you to."

Naomi suppressed a smile. Viola didn't have the authority of the bishop, but she liked to act as though she did.

Miriam hesitated.

"That sounds fair," Benjamin said. His brown eyes were warm and welcoming.

Naomi did not wait for Leah to protest. Her bare feet slapped the hardwood floor as she hurried across the living room, down the narrow hallway, and flung open the front door. A man stood with his back to her, holding his straw hat in his hands. His black coat was worn, the elbows threadbare. He looked to be of average height and build, but taller than Naomi. So far, he was nondescript, but still mysterious, which kept the butterflies fluttering in her stomach.

The man turned around. Naomi tried not to react. But he was as handsome as she had hoped he would be. And he definitely did not look like a hardened criminal. He had a boyish spray of freckles across a fair complexion and rich, reddish-brown hair. Best of all, he had clear blue eyes that gazed directly into hers. They were as calm and lovely as the ocean on a clear day.

Naomi was hooked. She needed to know all about this mysterious man who had shown up, out of the blue, on her doorstep. But Naomi was sure that her sisters—especially Miriam—were going to make that difficult. They had been keeping her on a tight rein after her last two courtships had ended in awkward breakups because she had been too trusting to see the warning signs that everyone else did. Fortunately, she had not fallen too hard for them. As it turned out, one was looking for a wife because he needed free childcare for his motherless children, and the other was just looking for casual fun, rather than a wife to love and cherish. But Naomi had not let that dim her expectations. She had read enough Amish romance novels to know that love was real and she deserved to experience it. And, if the dizzying emotion she was feeling right now were any indication, this just might be the man that she was going to fall for, no matter how much her family would fight it.

Gideon could see the judgment in the woman's eyes. No, it was worse than judgment. It was shock. She was staring up at him as if he had done something extraordinary. And maybe he had. She had probably never seen an Amish man with an arrest record before.

"You should *kumme* in," she said. She was standing in the threshold, holding the screen door open with her hip. She had a kind, open face and Gideon wanted to trust her. But he knew better than to expect sympathy. Most people who took him on as a hired hand treated him as an outsider, not as part of the family, especially after he was caught shoplifting. No one knew that his deepest longing was to have his own family and his own home. And not just any home—a farm. He wanted to support himself with good, honest work, on land that he could call his own. His parents had never been able to afford their own land. Like him, his father had lived hand to mouth, supporting the family on odd jobs and seasonal farmwork.

He glanced around at the quiet farmyard, where chickens pecked the damp earth, a large brindle-colored dog watched him from beneath the shade of an oak tree, and goats bleated from a pen beside a weathered, unpainted barn. He could be happy here, if they let him stay long enough to settle in. But that was not likely to happen.

The woman glanced over her shoulder, then back at Gideon. "Don't worry if my sister Miriam gives you a hard time. She can be a little…" She shook her head. "Just don't let her get to you. She means well, for certain sure. We're glad you here."

Gideon's brows drew together. "You are?"

"*Ya*, of course."

Her words made him feel a little spark of warmth inside.

"Just *kumme* on in," the woman said. "We'll talk about… everything."

Gideon sighed. The warm welcome would not last long.

"Oh, I'm Naomi, by the way. And my sisters are all waiting for us in the living room along with our brother, Benji. Let's see, there's also all the in-laws—John, Emma, David, and his parents and little sister, Katie—and the *bopplin*, Abby and Caleb. John and David are up in the south pasture with some of the goats and Emma is upstairs with the *bopplin*, so you'll meet them later.

"That's a big family."

Naomi flashed a smile. Gideon noticed the way it lit up

her face. "*Ya.* We like to say there's always room for one more at Stoneybrook Farm."

Gideon liked the sound of that. He was surprised at how comfortable he was starting to feel. Naomi had a way of putting him at ease. He was usually too shy to talk to people, preferring to listen and observe. Maybe this wouldn't be so bad, after all. Maybe the rest of the family would be just as welcoming. Except for Miriam, apparently.

Naomi stepped back to allow him room to come inside, then let the screen door bang shut behind them. He followed her down a hallway, into a spacious but plain living room that smelled of woodsmoke. The only wall decor was a calendar with a pastoral biblical scene. A handmade quilt lay across the back of a worn couch that faced a row of wooden chairs and a glider with embroidered cushions. A blue rag rug covered the scratched hardwood floor. In the corner of the room, there was a black potbellied stove with an orange glow behind the grate, a stack of wood, and a magazine rack stuffed with old copies of *The Budget* newspaper.

The room was full of strange faces. He wondered which one was the Miriam whom Naomi had warned him about. Probably the small, stout woman with the hardened expression and guarded eyes. She looked to be in her early thirties. Gideon tried to get out the word *hello*, but ended up just staring back at them.

Viola waved him over with her cane. "It's about time you came inside. Go ahead and tell them what you did, then let's get you settled in."

Gideon flinched.

"Maybe you'd like a gingersnap first?" a young woman asked. He guessed that she was in her early twenties. Her brown hair and eyes were a shade lighter than her siblings', who all had dark features and tanned skin. "I'm Leah. It's nice to meet you. I can get you *kaffi* too."

"No, thank you." He glanced at Viola. He just wanted to get this over with. Talking to people he knew was hard enough, but speaking to strangers—especially about his mistakes—was even worse.

"I'm Miriam Stoltzfus." Gideon had identified her correctly. "And that's Amanda." Miriam nodded toward a small, slim woman who couldn't be more than five feet tall. She held a gingersnap in one hand and waved with the other as she chewed, then smiled. "Nice to meet you."

"And I'm Benjamin," a man said. "Leah's twin brother." He had the same dark brown hair and eyes as most of the family. "You sure you don't want anything? These are *gut*." His plate with piled high with cookies.

"Uh, no thanks." Gideon looked down. It was hard to meet everyone's eyes. The room felt too hot, too stuffy. He didn't want coffee; he wanted a cold glass of ice water. But he didn't want to burden anyone by asking.

"*Vell*, go on and sit down and tell them about yourself," Viola said.

Gideon's stomach tightened, as if a belt were cinching around him. He took the straight-backed wooden chair beside Viola's glider. The room was quiet except for the sound of Amanda taking another bite of her cookie. Benjamin shifted his feet and Leah set down her coffee mug with a thump that sounded too loud in the silence. Gideon glanced up and saw Naomi staring at him. She gave an encouraging nod. "*Recht*. So, um… I came to Lancaster County trying to track down some relatives." Gideon looked down to study his hands as he spoke. "But it turned out to be a dead end. They jumped the fence a while back and are living as *Englisch* now. They moved to Hawaii, so…"

"So, you don't have anybody," Benjamin said.

Gideon didn't know how to respond, so he just kept staring down at his hands.

"And he doesn't have a job or a home, either," Viola said.

Gideon appreciated that she was sticking up for him, but her straightforward way of doing it stung.

"Are you trying to get back to Holmes County?" Miriam asked. "That's where you're from, ain't so?"

"*Ya*. I could go back." Gideon shrugged. "Or I could stay here. It doesn't make much difference. My last job out there ended, so there's nothing waiting for me there." And nothing for him here either. Maybe this would be the time and place when *Gott* answered his prayer to belong.

Gideon cut the thought short. Dreaming would only lead to disappointment. So far, it had not been *Gott*'s will for him to have a place of his own. He was prepared to accept that for as long as he had to. He just wished it wasn't so hard.

"And, you got into some trouble back in Holmes County?" Bishop Amos nodded at Gideon.

Gideon glanced up just long enough to see that Amos's eyes were kind and soft. He swallowed hard. "I got caught stealing."

There was a sharp intake of breath across the room. He didn't look, but felt sure it was Miriam. Getting arrested for shoplifting wasn't something that happened in Amish communities. But he had been between jobs and hungry. He knew that he should not have taken the sandwich from the deli but, in a moment of weakness, he had. Before she died of cancer, Gideon's mother used to say that pride cometh before destruction and a haughty spirit before a fall. She was right, he had been too prideful to ask his church district for a handout.

But it was more than that. He had also been too ashamed.

Since his father died in a farming accident when he was thirteen, and his mother passed away less than a year later, Gideon had lived hand to mouth, trying to make himself useful enough to earn his keep in other people's homes. By now, he should have a home of his own, a family of his own. But he was still trying to make ends meet. Maybe it was that he was still struggling to find solid ground after he lost his parents. Or maybe he had just had a string of bad luck, with no one to help him get back on track after unexpected expenses, like the medical bill from an emergency appendectomy that had taken him five years to pay off, even after his church district pitched in as much as they could. Whatever the reason, it wasn't a lack of trying. He was a hard worker, that much he knew.

But now, he had to face a new family, in a new home that wasn't his, and try to justify his past. They would see him as a drifter, perhaps even a criminal. It seemed like the harder he tried, the more he failed to earn anyone's approval. Except for Viola and Amos. For some reason the elderly woman had taken him under her wing when she heard about him from her niece in the Little Creek church district, given him a chance, and convinced her bishop to do the same. But that made him feel even more pressure. He didn't want to let her down.

"*Vell*, what did you steal?" Miriam asked. "And why?"

"Food from a grocery store. After I got caught, I had to go through the *Englisch* court system, but it's all over now. As soon as my probation ended, I decided to come here."

"To get away from people who knew?" Miriam asked.

Gideon wished that she would not be so direct, but he did not blame her. She had to vet a stranger before letting him live on her property. "I guess you could say that." He tried to gather his thoughts. "I wanted to try someplace new, hoped things might work out better." He cleared his throat. "Things haven't worked out for me so good, I guess you could say. So when I learned that I had some cousins in Lancaster County, I headed straight here."

Viola clapped her hands together. "So," she said. "That's that. The poor *bu* was hungry, so he stole something to eat. He's repented. And it wasn't much of a crime to begin with." She shook her head. "He shouldn't have gotten probation for it. But that's the *Englisch* for you. Now, let's get him moved in."

Miriam studied Gideon without responding.

"Viola's *recht*," Naomi said. "He can take the little storage room where John slept before he and Leah got married and they moved into the new addition that he built."

Miriam took a deep breath and let it out slowly. Gideon watched her as she thought things over.

"It's a *gut* idea," Benjamin said. "I could use an extra hand around here. John's always busy with a building project or repair work and now that we've combined our herd with David's, there's a lot more work to do with the goats."

"That's true," Amanda said. "We could use the help."

"You're missing the point," Naomi said. "Gideon needs a home." She turned to look at him with those deep brown eyes. "You don't have any place else to go and no one else to turn to, ain't so?"

"*Nee*." He said the word quietly and almost dropped eye contact, but managed to hold it. Her gaze was so warm, so welcoming.

No one said it out loud, but it was clear that he did not have any money either. After the $17.98 in his pocket was gone, he would be completely broke. Again. Traveling to Lancaster County had wiped him out. But the disappointment barely registered. All he felt now was resigned and numb.

"Do you need to talk it over with the rest of the family?" Bishop Amos asked.

"They won't have a problem with it," Miriam said.

"Emma will definitely be on board," Benjamin said.

"And so will David," Amanda said.

"And John," Leah added.

Amos rubbed his chin. "That just leaves you, Miriam."

Miriam nodded. "We won't turn him away. But there isn't room for him in the house. That storage room is too small."

Gideon felt pretty sure that she was making an excuse, since John had stayed there, apparently.

"But since David's parents are visiting a sick relative in Pinecraft for the next two weeks, he can stay in their *dawdi hous*." Miriam turned to Gideon. "David's little sister, Katie, lives there too, but she's moved into the house with us while her parents are gone. They didn't want her to miss school."

Gideon didn't want to ask what would happen after they got back. Most likely he would be out on the street again, looking for work.

"After that, we might not have a place for you," Miriam said.

Right. Just as he had predicted. She would not want him to stick around after the two weeks were over. But it would appease her bishop to give him a chance. She could say that she tried, but it didn't work out, then send him on his way.

"Miriam—" Naomi said before her sister cut her off.

"We can talk about it later," Miriam said.

"You don't know what I was going to say," Naomi said.

Miriam raised an eyebrow.

Naomi crossed her arms and looked away from her sister, directly at Gideon. Her eyes sparked with emotion. He could imagine getting to know Naomi, tending the goats with her, helping with the milking, hitching up the buggy for her. He wanted to walk the pastureland by her side while she told him about herself. He wanted her to ask him to stay after the two weeks were up.

But those were dangerous thoughts. He had not had a close friend in a long time and he shouldn't be looking to make one now. Two weeks, and he would be on his way. Maybe with enough money to make it back to Holmes County. While he was here, he would guard his heart, keep his head down, and avoid Naomi as best he could. Anything else would lead to heartbreak. He could not allow himself to give in to his emotions, no matter how much he longed to form a connection with someone just like Naomi.

Chapter Two

After the family scattered for afternoon chores, Naomi wanted to follow Gideon out to the *dawdi hous* and pepper him with questions. She sensed that there was so much more to his story than he had shared. She was captivated by the mystery—and by those expressive blue eyes. Especially since he was so taciturn and aloof. But Miriam grabbed her elbow as she started for the door.

"Hold on," Miriam said.

Naomi turned to see that Miriam's face was set in tight lines. Well, that wasn't unusual. Her oldest *schwester* always found something to get worked up about. She was too serious and reserved. Naomi understood that she'd had to harden herself to get their family through those difficult, early years after their parents' sudden death. But, enough was enough. Naomi longed for Miriam—all her sisters, really—to stop being so tough. It was okay to be open and to express emotion. But they preferred to hold their feelings inside and put up a strong front. Worst of all, they looked down on her because they thought she wasn't strong. Naomi thought that feeling and sharing emotions did take strength. But she was the only one.

Naomi sighed. "What?"

"Where are you hurrying off to?"

"I'm just going to help Gideon settle in."

"Benji can do that."

"And so can I."

Now it was Miriam's turn to sigh. "You don't want to seem too eager."

"I'm just being friendly. We're Amish. We're supposed to be hospitable, especially to a *bruder* in need."

"You sure you're just being friendly? As Amish we're also supposed to maintain a certain amount of distance with young men."

Naomi stuck her hands on her hips. "I've never crossed any lines before, and you know it."

"That Aaron boy tried when he was courting you."

"*Ya*, and I gave him a piece of my mind."

Miriam's lips curved into an almost imperceptible smile. "I was proud of you for that."

"I'm not afraid to stand up for myself. Same as the rest of us."

"*Recht*, but…"

"But what?" Naomi's eyes narrowed.

"*Vell*, you weren't interested in Aaron. But what if you had had a crush on him? What might have happened then? Or what might have happened with Ezekiel?"

"Ezekiel was old—nearly thirty-two. I wasn't interested."

"I know, but what if you had been?"

"He just wanted a free nanny for his *kinner*."

"It's *gut* you saw that…eventually. You were taken in by all the attention at first. If you remember, it took us pointing it out for you to see it. You could have been stuck in a bad marriage for life, with a man who just wanted to take advantage of your good nature."

"Miriam, we've been over this."

"And we're going to go over it again. You're so eager to fall in love that one of these days you might end up with the wrong man."

"And you're afraid that's going to be Gideon?"

Miriam lifted her hands, palms up. "Could be."

"Miriam, I'm an adult."

"And the older you get, the more desperate you are. I know you feel left behind, since your courtships fell through."

Crashed and burned was a better description but Naomi was not about to make that clarification. "Stop treating me like a *kind*. I'm perfectly capable of choosing a *gut* match."

"Then prove it."

Naomi flung up her hands. "I am. Am I running around with some *bu* right now? *Nee*. I've never done anything wrong!"

"It's not you that I'm worried about. It's men who might not have honorable intentions. You might not see it, so I have to make sure that you do."

"You're not my *mamm*, Miriam, as much as you like to tell me what to do."

Miriam's expression hardened. Then she turned away. "We'll talk later." Her sister cleared the empty plates and mugs from the coffee table. "Just keep your distance from Gideon, please. We don't need any trouble. I wouldn't have invited him to stay if I didn't think it was *oll recht*, but why take any chances? We don't know enough about him. And he does have a criminal record."

"It doesn't count. Didn't you hear the story?"

"*Ya*. And I'm sure it's the truth—"

Naomi's eyes narrowed. "You always say that when you're actually not so sure. You don't believe him?"

"I didn't say that. All I'm saying is that we don't know him. There's nothing wrong with being careful. I want to do the right thing and help him out, but I also have to keep our family safe."

"I can keep myself safe."

Miriam exhaled, and headed out of the room with the stack of dishes. "I sure hope so," she murmured.

"I heard that."

"*Gut*. You should know that I'm not trying to hurt you."

"*Vell*, try or not, you are." Naomi said the words under her breath, so that Miriam did not hear. She and Miriam were such opposites that it was hard not to clash with her. But Naomi always felt bad afterward. She knew that her sister had sacrificed her own happiness for the family's sake—including the suitor she had planned to marry. Their parents' death had set Miriam's life on an unexpected path, derailing the engagement.

Naomi knew that she should apologize to Miriam for saying that she wasn't her *mamm*. But right now, Naomi was too upset. She needed to walk outside, get some fresh air, and calm down. And if she happened to run into a handsome stranger in the farmyard, well, that couldn't be helped.

Gideon was overwhelmed as he stood in front of the *dawdi haus*, staring at the sturdy little structure. He had never lived alone in his own house, with all the space just to himself. The building looked newly built, with a fresh coat of white paint and a welcoming front porch, just big enough for two rocking chairs. There were two spacious windows on the first floor, a small dormer window centered above them, and all of it topped off by a shiny tin roof.

Benjamin trotted up the front porch steps and opened the door. "*Kumme* in," he said as he disappeared inside.

Gideon slung his green duffel bag over his shoulder and followed. The interior smelled of fresh paint and newly sawed wood. Sunlight shone through the windows and fell across the hardwood floors, making the space feel cheery and airy, despite the small size. Everything was warm and bright, with whitewashed walls and colorful quilts folded over the furniture.

Benjamin showed him that the house was divided into two rooms: a living area with a kitchenette that had a woodstove with burners on top for cooking, and a bedroom with a double bed and washbasin on a wooden stand. Benjamin motioned to a staircase that was almost as steep as a ladder. "There's another bedroom in the attic loft. That's Katie's room. But you'll have the whole place to yourself until…" Benjamin cut himself off.

Gideon knew that he had been about to mention the deadline that Miriam had set, but had stopped short. "Uh, *vell*, *danki*. This place is *wunderbar*."

"I helped build it." Benjamin flashed a sheepish grin. "*Oll recht*, John did most of it. He worked construction before he married Leah and knows all about it."

Gideon nodded. He wasn't sure what to say. Benjamin was friendly and disarming, but that almost made Gideon more uncomfortable. He wasn't sure how to be friendly back, not when he felt so self-conscious being a stranger among a close-knit family. Fortunately, they were interrupted before Gideon had to respond. A baby's wails drifted through the walls, followed by footsteps pounding across the porch and a knock on the door.

"*Kumme* in," Benjamin shouted.

The door swung open to reveal a woman with honey-blond hair, green eyes, and flushed cheeks. An infant squirmed and cried in her arms. "Hi. You must be Gideon," she said loudly enough to be heard over the baby's howling. "I'm Benji's *frau*, Emma." She looked down at the child and shook her head, but kept the smile on her face. "And this is Caleb. His real name is Benjamin, but that's too confusing. You know how it is in Amish families. We tried calling him Benjamin's Benjamin, but that was confusing too. So, we called him Caleb's Benjamin, after Benji's late *daed*, but that got shortened pretty quick to just plain Caleb."

Gideon knew lots of Amish folks with nicknames that tied them to a relative. That way, you could tell people apart by showing who they belonged to. Some families had three or four people with the same first name. His father had been called Gideon too, so Gideon's nickname used to be Gideon's Gideon. It was a mouthful, but Gideon had liked it. He wanted to tell Emma that, but it felt too personal and he was afraid it wouldn't come out right. So, after a moment he said, "Nice to meet you. And you too, Caleb." He smiled. The baby squeezed his eyes shut and wailed.

"You want me to take him?" Benjamin asked.

"*Ya*." Emma let out a deep breath as she and Benjamin made eye contact. "I was hoping you could. I need a break."

"Sure. I need to check on those sick nanny goats, but he can *kumme* to the barn with me. We'll get him settled down." Benjamin laughed. "Eventually."

"I'll go help get dinner on." Emma passed Caleb to Benjamin, stood on her tiptoes, and kissed him on the cheek. Gideon felt a pang of longing for the closeness of a relationship like that. What would it feel like to have someone who cared about you? Someone who shared your good days and bad, who held your hand as you walked through life together?

He dropped his duffel bag onto the living room floor and they all headed outside together, into the afternoon sunshine. The air smelled of earth and pine. "Let me know what I can do to help," Gideon said as he followed Benjamin across the farmyard. The dirt felt soft and familiar under his work boots. They headed toward a goat pen beside an old, unpainted barn. Gideon liked the weathered look of the building. It felt old-fashioned and quaint, like something out of olden times. Not like the bright red *Englisch* barns.

"First thing, I've got to—"

A loud honk interrupted Benjamin. Gideon spun around to see a goose sprinting toward them with wings flapping. Her flat, orange feet threw up a cloud of dust as she cut across the yard.

"Belinda!" Benjamin tried to wave the goose away, but she kept charging straight for Gideon.

"Bad goose!" Benjamin shouted. "Don't bite him!"

Gideon resisted the urge to flinch. He knew what he needed to do and slowly lowered himself onto one knee, against his instincts, which told him to run to avoid a painful nip. The goose flapped her wings in a big show of confidence, thrust her head forward, and hissed. "Easy now," Gideon whispered. "We're all friends here, ain't so?" He let his hands drop to his sides, as nonthreatening as possible. "It's *oll recht*."

The goose honked again, then tilted her head and stared at him through glittering black eyes. "That's better." Gideon's voice was soft and soothing. "Let's be friends." They watched one another for a moment. Then the goose ruffled her feathers and strutted away.

"Sorry about that," Benjamin said. "Belinda's our guard goose and she takes her job seriously." Caleb was still crying softly and Benjamin adjusted his hold on him. "Not sure how you managed that. She doesn't usually stop once she's started an attack."

Gideon stood up, brushed off his knees, and shrugged. "I just like animals, is all."

"And they seem to like you."

Gideon glanced over at Belinda. She was marching back and forth in front of the feed trough, like a good little soldier.

"I hope so." He nodded toward the goats in the pen. "What can I do to help you out?"

"*Vell*, you could get Caleb to calm down so I could give the sick goats their medicine." Benjamin chuckled as he headed toward the pen with Caleb still tucked in his arms.

"Sure."

"*Ach*, I was joking."

"Oh." Gideon felt his face heat up. Of course Benjamin would not trust him to hold his son.

Benjamin flashed a grin. "But if you don't mind…"

"Not at all." Gideon had always gotten on well with babies. They didn't ask questions or judge. They just trusted and loved.

"*Gut*. It'll be easier for me to tend to the goats than to tell you what to do. I'm not so *gut* with explaining things."

So Benjamin didn't always feel comfortable talking either. Gideon hoped he might fit in after all—a little bit, at least. Caleb whimpered as Benjamin slid him into Gideon's arms. Then the baby sniffled, took a deep breath, and howled.

"You're *oll recht*," Gideon said.

Benjamin hesitated. "I can take him back if you want me to. He's teething, so he's been real fussy lately."

"*Nee*, we're going to be fine." Gideon looked down at Caleb's scrunched-up, little red face. "Ain't so?"

Benjamin jogged over to the goat pen and unlatched the gate. "I'll try to hurry," he called over his shoulder.

Gideon moved Caleb to his shoulder and patted his back as he walked the farmyard. "You're okay, little guy," he murmured as they passed the big brindled-colored dog dozing in the shade of a red wheelbarrow. "It's not so bad, is it?" The dog opened his eyes and thumped his tail against the ground as they passed. "Just look at this big, beautiful world, Caleb." They reached the white fence at the edge of the farmyard.

Gideon knew that Bishop Amos and his wife, Edna, lived down the hill on the other side, in the tidy little farmhouse with the kitchen garden alongside it. In the valley beyond their house, there was a field of yellow sunflowers next to a pond of silver water that caught the sun and sparkled.

Gideon turned to pace in the opposite direction, toward the farmhouse. The old, weathered structure had a double front porch—one on top of the other—and a tin roof. It must have been in the shape of a big box originally, but it looked like there had been a series of additions over the years, giving it a haphazard, lived-in appearance, just right for a big, boisterous family. Gideon sighed. He could imagine all the lively discussions over a home-cooked meal, the cozy evenings by the woodstove while the men flipped through the latest copy of *The Budget* newspaper and the women knitted. He could imagine sitting on the couch beside Naomi—No. He would not let his mind wander there. Naomi was a sweet young woman. With plenty of prospects, for certain sure. She would never be interested in him.

Gideon realized that Caleb was not crying anymore. He looked down and saw that he was fast asleep. Gideon felt a rush of warm satisfaction. At least Caleb had taken to him. And the goose, but that didn't really count.

The screen door slammed and Gideon glanced up to see Naomi bounding down the porch steps. Her *kapp* strings flew behind her and her eyes sparkled. She was so full of energy, so full of life. He felt himself grinning as he watched her.

"Hey!" she shouted in a stage whisper. "I can't believe you got Caleb to go to sleep!"

Gideon could not hide his smile. He was not used to compliments. Especially from enthusiastic young women who looked like they meant what they said. He gave a sheepish shrug. "*Ya*, I guess so."

"Just wait until Miriam hears about this."

Gideon's smile dropped back to a frown. He was pretty sure that Miriam would not be impressed. It would take a lot more than this to convince her to let him stay. But maybe if he got on well with the rest of the family, they could outvote her.

Or maybe not.

"You better not risk putting him down. I'll give you a tour of the farm while you hold him."

Gideon's smile returned. That sounded like a perfect plan. Just him and Naomi. Then he remembered to keep his distance, for both their sakes. Miriam would never let him stay if she thought that he was sweet on her little sister. "Come on," she said without slowing down. "We'll let Benji know."

Benjamin looked up from a bucket of feed when he saw them. "Hey, you got Caleb to settle down."

"Pretty impressive, ain't so?" Naomi said.

"For certain sure. And did he tell you about Belinda?"

"*Nee*. What happened?"

"He made friends with her."

"Already?"

Benjamin nodded as he scooped out a cup of the feed. "*Ya*."

Naomi turned to Gideon. "She didn't try to bite you?"

"*Vell*, she tried. But…" He shrugged. "I guess she changed her mind."

"Belinda doesn't change her mind. You must have a way with animals."

"And *boppli* too, apparently," Benjamin added as he snapped the plastic lid back onto the feed bucket.

"Speaking of which, we're going to keep walking with Caleb so he doesn't wake up," Naomi said. "We'll be around."

"Oll recht. Danki."

They wandered across the farmyard, side by side. "Over

there, behind the house, is the production building." She pointed to a big, industrial-looking structure made of sheet metal. "We pasteurize and store the goat milk in there. And there's a little office inside too. Leah does most of the office work. She took a business class to learn how to do all that."

"And up there," she said, "is where the goats forage. We rotate them between pastures. Amanda and David are almost always up there with them, or in the goat shed." Gideon studied the sweeping view of fields and pastureland that spread out in a carpet of rich green, dotted by blue wildflowers. The goats looked like miniature plushies in the distance. A high-pitched whistle carried on the wind and two black-and-white border collies swept around the herd. He couldn't make out the details, but he could see the swift, eager movement and hear the bleating of the goats carried on the warm breeze. The scent of damp earth drifted down with the noise. Gideon inhaled deeply. He liked it here, on this big beautiful farm, with this friendly woman, who seemed to care.

"Tell me about yourself," she said as she studied the movement of the dogs circling the goats.

Gideon paused. He was not sure how to answer. "Why?" he asked. He hoped that was not a rude response. But he didn't understand why she was asking.

The wind picked up and blew the skirt of her dress. She held it down and turned to look at him. "Because I want to know."

"Oh." Gideon still didn't know what to say.

Naomi smiled. "It's okay. It's not a trick question."

"Oh." He realized that he had repeated himself, cleared his throat, and looked down.

"There's something about you," Naomi said. She let her smile fade as she studied him with intense eyes.

"There is?"

"Caleb doesn't calm down for just anybody. You're a baby whisperer."

"And a goose whisperer."

Naomi laughed. "That's right."

"So what makes you the way you are?"

"Uh, *vell*… That's a pretty big question."

Naomi smiled and looked away. "*Ya*, that might have been a little much of me. I hear that a lot."

"That you're too much?"

"Ya."

"I don't think so."

Naomi's eyes darted to his. "Really?"

"Really. And that was a *gut* question…" Gideon wanted to reassure her. The problem was him, not her. He had been too insecure to answer her.

"It was?"

He smiled. "*Ya*."

Their eyes stayed locked on one another. Gideon could hear his heart beat in his chest and feel the soft breeze on his skin. He was acutely aware of every sound, every feeling. He had not felt this alive in a long time.

A door opened and slammed shut.

They both jerked their attention to the noise behind them. Miriam was striding out of an enclosed porch on the back of the house. Her expression was guarded, but Gideon knew how to read people well enough to pick up on the tension around her eyes and mouth.

His stomach sank. He should not have let himself feel that connection with Naomi. Keeping his place at Stoneybrook Farm had to be his priority.

This was not the time or place to open his heart.

Chapter Three

"Emma and I need some help with supper," Miriam said to Naomi.

"I'm busy." Of course Miriam would come along now, of all times, when she was just starting to break the ice with Gideon. When she had locked eyes with him, he might have felt the connection too. There could be something there, waiting to be nurtured.

"There's work to be done."

Naomi flashed a smile. "I'm doing the work of hospitality."

Gideon shifted his weight from one foot to the other. Caleb stirred in his arms and Miriam's attention shot to the baby.

"I was, uh, giving Benjamin a break so he could tend to the goats," Gideon said.

"Oh. *Danki.* That's…a surprise."

Gideon's brow crinkled and he looked down to study Caleb's tuft of soft blond hair.

Naomi raised her eyebrows. "Because it's so hard to get him to settle down when he's teething. That's what you meant, right, Miriam?"

"Of course that's what I meant. What else would I have meant?"

That you didn't expect a criminal to be sweet enough

to soothe a baby. Naomi didn't say the words out loud, but she shot Miriam a look that showed she had picked up on the truth.

Miriam frowned. "We appreciate it, Gideon."

Gideon nodded. "It's no problem. I'll go back to the goat pen now and see what else I can do for Benjamin."

Naomi wanted to tell him to wait, but he was gone before she could speak. She had been trying to think of how to convince him to finish their conversation without sounding too forward, since that's what Miriam accused her of being.

"Let him get back to work," Miriam said as soon as Gideon was out of earshot.

"I didn't say anything," Naomi said.

"You wanted to."

"You can't read minds, you know."

Miriam cracked a smile and nudged Naomi with her elbow. "Want to bet?"

Naomi rolled her eyes.

"I can see you watching him, you know."

Naomi jerked her gaze away from Gideon as her face heated up. She was sure that she was blushing, so she turned her face away and pretended to adjust her *kapp*.

"Let's go inside and get supper on," Miriam said.

"I know that's just an excuse to get me away from Gideon."

"*Vell*, someone has to do the cooking."

Naomi sighed. "Fine."

"You like to cook. You're always talking about all the things you want to cook for your husband and *kinner* one day."

Naomi almost said that if she was going to have a husband, then she had to talk to eligible young men first, but she kept silent. "I don't like to be interrupted."

"And what exactly did I interrupt?" Miriam's hands moved to her hips.

"Nothing." Except for that intriguing moment when she gazed into Gideon's clear blue eyes and—

"Then there's no problem."

"*Nee*. None at all."

Movement caught Naomi's attention and she looked up to see Amanda striding down the hillside, arms swinging by her sides. "You haven't been up there long," Naomi shouted.

Amanda broke into a jog and arrived in the backyard with her face glowing from exertion, smelling like fresh air and newly cut grass. She wore an old blue work kerchief over her dark brown hair and her apron was smudged with dirt. "*Ya*, I had to find out what was happening."

"What do you mean?" Naomi asked.

"With you and Gideon."

"Nothing was happening with me and Gideon."

"I saw you two talking," Amanda said.

Naomi threw up her hands. "Are you serious? This is *lecherich*."

"It's not ridiculous. You two were walking alone, deep in conversation…" Amanda hesitated. "You're not… I mean…"

"I don't know what you're getting at."

"You're not sweet on him, are you?" Amanda asked.

"*Nee*! Of course not."

"She barely knows him," Miriam said. "She can't be sweet on him yet." But Miriam's expression looked as though that was exactly what she thought was happening too.

Naomi shot Miriam a look. "*Vell*, how can I get to know him if you *kumme* outside and chase him away as soon as we start talking?"

Miriam narrowed her eyes. "So you *were* trying to get to know him."

"I can't win with you." Naomi shook her head. "I'm going inside." She turned around and saw Emma and Leah standing on the other side of the wall of windows that lined the enclosed back porch. They were both staring intently. As soon as she caught them, they flinched and turned away. "You have got to be kidding me!" Naomi shouted as she stormed across the backyard and tore open the screen door. "You've been watching me too?"

Emma bit her lip. Leah glanced at Emma, then back at Naomi. "Um, *ya*."

Naomi exhaled. "There was nothing to see."

Leah and Emma exchanged another look.

"Wait, how long were you spying us?"

"The whole time?" Leah said, as if she were asking a question.

"Really? The whole time we've been out here?"

"Ya."

"Miriam too?"

"Of course," Leah said.

"He seems nice," Emma said. Naomi wasn't surprised to hear Emma put in a good word for Gideon. She had gotten into her own trouble during *rumspringa*, before she repented and fell in love with Benjamin.

"He is." Naomi felt herself smile as she said it.

"*Ach, nee*," Miriam said from the doorway. "That look on your face. Please tell me that you are not getting any ideas, Naomi."

"Pffft. I'm not getting ideas."

"You don't even know him yet." Amanda stood on her tiptoes to peer around Miriam, who blocked the doorway. "Don't let yourself get carried away."

"Pretty sure we just went over this. You all aren't letting me get to know him."

"You'll have a *gut* opportunity over dinner tonight," Miriam said. "Or after the church service tomorrow." Chaperoned opportunity, was what Miriam meant. Naomi didn't want to do anything more than talk to Gideon—okay, she wouldn't mind if he eventually gave her a little kiss, but that would be far in the future. Well, maybe not *that* far in the future. But she didn't need a chaperone. It was perfectly acceptable to go out alone in courting buggies.

"Naomi, are you listening?" Miriam was leaning against the doorframe, staring at her.

"What?"

"Just don't get ahead of yourself."

"I never do."

They all shot her the same look. Naomi deflated a little bit. It was true, she did have a tendency to get carried away, especially in matters of the heart. But what was so wrong with that? Why shouldn't she want to fall in love, get married, have lots of babies, and live happily ever after?

"*Vell*, that chicken potpie isn't going to bake itself," Miriam said. "We best get to it."

Ten minutes later, as she rolled out a piecrust, Naomi decided it was time to bring up Gideon again. Miriam just needed a little nudge to see things clearly. Naomi should be able to do that. "You know," she said as she leaned into the rolling pin. "Gideon sure is *gut* with Caleb. I think you have to be a *gut* person to calm a baby like that. They have to feel safe with you. And he made friends with Belinda right away."

Miriam sprinkled some flour onto Naomi's piecrust.

"The dough isn't sticking," Naomi said. "You don't need to do that."

"What's that, then?" Miriam pointed and Naomi saw where the dough was pressed against the wooden rolling pin.

Naomi pursed her lips as she peeled it off. "Fine. Maybe just a little bit."

"Anyway," Miriam said. "It was thoughtful of him to take

Caleb while Benjamin tended to the goats and Emma took a break from all the crying."

Naomi gave a triumphant nod. "Exactly."

"But Caleb might have fallen asleep because he had worn himself out with all that fussing. It might have just been *gut* timing."

Leah handed a teething biscuit to her five-month-old stepdaughter, Abby, who sat in a baby seat in the middle of the kitchen table. "Both the *bopplin* have been crying themselves to sleep lately."

"I think it shows that Gideon's got a sweet nature," Naomi said.

Miriam sighed. "Maybe. But there's no reason to jump to conclusions."

"Either way," Naomi added.

"Either way," Miriam agreed. "Let's just give it time."

Naomi gave a mischievous smile. "You're right."

Miriam stopped, set down the flour sifter in her hand, and stared at Naomi. "*Vell*, I never thought I'd hear you say that."

"Taking the time to know someone requires spending time with them," Naomi pointed out.

A few beats ticked by before Miriam nodded and set the sifter back on the shelf. "I agree."

Naomi's smile became a grin. "You do?"

"*Ya*. I'll do the chores with him tomorrow to get to know him better. That's a *gut* idea, Naomi."

Naomi's grin evaporated. Miriam was not going to make this easy.

Gideon met the rest of the family when he and Benjamin came in for supper. Leah's husband, John, was large-framed and surprisingly tall—Gideon estimated around six foot four. He looked even bigger when standing beside Amanda and Miriam, who were very petite. "We're glad to have you here," John said with a firm and hearty handshake. Miriam had mentioned that John had lived in the spare room, so he must have been an outsider too, once. The thought gave Gideon a small dash of confidence.

A skinny girl with freckles covering her face and arms came bounding into the room just as they were pulling out their chairs. She waved a piece of paper in the air and grinned. "I drew a picture of our house. Want to see it?"

"Sure we do," a man said as he followed her into the dining room. "Sorry we're running late," he added.

"I was helping to bring in the goats from the south pasture," the girl said. "I did Amanda's job today."

Amanda smiled. "*Ya*, *danki* for covering for me. I came in early to…" She glanced at Naomi, who glared back at her. "Help with supper."

Gideon knew that Miriam had used that as an excuse to get Naomi away from him earlier that day. They must have all been involved, one way or another. This family had their very own mini Amish telegraph, for certain sure. That meant they were keeping a close eye on him. Well, that was fine, because he would never give them any reason for concern. But he didn't like being the center of attention. It made him feel itchy. He rubbed the back of his neck and turned to the newcomers. "I'm Gideon. Nice to meet you both."

"And I'm David. Nice to meet you too," the man said as he pulled out a chair. "I heard you'll be staying with us for a couple weeks."

Gideon noticed right away that David had specified the time period. He wondered if they were all talking about that deadline and how they would make sure that he left as soon as it was up.

"Don't forget about me!" the little girl piped up.

"*Recht*." David tousled her hair and she gave him a playful shove with her elbow. "This is my ten-year-old sister, Katie."

"I need to show everyone this," she said. Her smile lit up the room as she bounced up from her chair and held up the picture.

David leaned forward to see the crayon drawing. "You've got all our bedrooms there."

The drawing looked like a dollhouse, with the wall cut away to show all the rooms within.

"Yep. Since I can't draw us, I drew where we each live. This one is yours," she said and pointed to a room with lop-sided furniture.

"That's a *gut*-looking room for a *gut*-looking man," David said.

Amanda laughed. "For certain sure. Nice job, Katie."

"Look, I even drew your straw hat on the wall." The hat was the same size as the dresser.

"*Vell*, my head might not be quite that big," David said.

"That's what you think," Amanda said.

David smoothed down his hair and grinned.

"Look," Katie said as she pointed at each of the rooms, one by one. "They're all there."

"I know whose that one is," Leah said and pointed to the room with an extra-long pair of pants hanging on a peg on the wall.

John chuckled. "I sure do stick out in this family."

Gideon felt a pang of envy. Even though John said he stuck out, it was clear he belonged.

"Uh-oh." Katie frowned and turned the paper so that she could see it. "Gideon doesn't have a room in the picture."

"That's okay," Gideon said. He didn't like the look of frustration in Katie's eyes. He knew what it was like to try to do something and feel like a failure. "I'm not… I'm not part of the family. I'm just passing through." He tried to sound nonchalant, but the words stuck in his throat. He wished that he did have a room among theirs. He'd like to see his belongings with the rest of theirs, even if Katie made his hat too big or his pants too long. He wanted to be close enough to them that they could point out what was funny about him and all chuckle together.

Gideon noticed Miriam and Naomi watching him, instead of looking at the picture. He wondered if he had said the wrong thing. He wanted so badly to stay at Stoneybrook Farm, and not just pass through, but he didn't want to embarrass himself by making it obvious that he wanted to overstay his welcome. He decided he had said what he needed to, especially when Katie gave a solemn nod and said, "*Gut*. I was afraid it wasn't good enough."

"It certain sure is," Gideon said. "It's just right."

The room fell into the low hum of side conversations. "Hey, Miriam," Benjamin said loudly enough to be heard above the din. "Hurry up and say the blessing so we can eat. I'm starving." She led them in a silent prayer, then the room erupted with the clanging of silverware, animated voices, and the occasional cry of a baby.

Gideon was not used to the loud, boisterous conversation around the dinner table. It all seemed to be good-hearted, but it was still a lot to take in. He sat quietly in the spacious dining room, observing everyone and wondering what it would be like to belong to a big, extended family. As he listened, he studied the tall farmhouse windows and the handsewn place mats that looked like miniature quilts. Whenever he shifted in his chair, the old wooden floor creaked. He liked the coziness of the well-worn house.

The meal was a delicious chicken potpie with a golden-brown flaky crust. He tried not to let his attention linger on

Naomi between bites. Someone might notice. But more than that, he needed to keep his distance. He picked up his glass of iced tea, took a long, slow sip, and stole a glance in her direction. She was staring directly at him.

Gideon jerked his attention away, then flicked his eyes back up to see if she was still looking at him. She was not. Her eyes were on her plate and her face had flushed red. Gideon tried very hard not to look at her again. He wasn't sure why he wanted to in the first place. He had been alone for so many years that it had become second nature to him. He could not afford a *frau* or *kinner*, so he had not courted anyone. It felt good to be responsible, to not make promises he couldn't keep. But as he looked down at his plate, fighting the urge to glance back up at Naomi, he was tempted not to be so responsible anymore.

Would it be so terrible to try to form a connection, even though he wasn't financially secure? Yes, it would be. He had to stay strong and keep trying his best to do the right thing.

"So, Gideon, how long have you been in Bluebird Hills?" a voice asked.

Gideon looked up from his plate. The low hum of conversation stopped abruptly as they all waited for him to answer. Gideon studied the faces for a moment, trying to form the right answer. He didn't like speaking to groups of people. Talking one-on-one felt less intimidating.

"And how did you meet Viola Esch?" Amanda asked. "She didn't really explain that."

Gideon nodded and took a big sip of his drink. That gave him time to think while he swallowed. He patted his mouth with a cloth napkin and tucked it back in his lap. "*Vell*, uh, I got here a few days ago. Just long enough to track down my kinfolk and learn that they aren't here anymore." Gideon remembered the way his heart had fluttered during the long bus ride down the endless ribbon of black pavement. By the time he reached Lancaster County, he could hardly bear the anticipation. That hope had only made it harder when he found out that he was still alone.

"And what happened then?" Benjamin asked. Caleb was dozing on the floor in a bouncy seat and Benjamin kept tapping it with the toe of his shoe to keep it moving. "How did you meet Viola?"

Gideon flicked through all the things he might say until he landed on something that felt right. "Um, I had been going around the Little Creek church district, asking questions, trying to find those relatives, and she got wind of it."

"Viola's always the first to hear anything on the Amish telegraph," Leah said as she held Abby in her lap, feeding her bites from her own plate. A round of laughter passed through the room. John leaned over and picked up a green pea that the baby had dropped on the floor, then patted her chubby knee. Leah glanced over at him and beamed. Gideon could feel the warmth around the table, among the couples. But it was like watching from outside a window on a cold winter's day. He was standing in a steely wind, while the others sat around a cozy, crackling fire.

Gideon could remember being on the other side of that window, long ago, when his parents were still alive. They had not had much, but they had had each other. And in the quiet evenings after his father came home from doing odd jobs or working someone else's farm, they would all gather around the woodstove. His father would read to him from a book of illustrated Bible stories while his mother knitted, her rocking chair creaking back and forth in a gentle, familiar rhythm.

His chest contracted at the memory and he shoved it away. It was better to push everything down than feel the loss. He thought about Naomi, sitting across the table from him with those lively brown eyes and eager smile. Her family's disapproval wasn't the only reason that he had to keep her at arm's length. He had to protect himself from losing what he loved. Because if he ever made it into that cozy, warm place again—where he felt seen and loved—he would not be able to bear losing it once more.

Chapter Four

Naomi tried to focus on cooking breakfast, but her eyes kept wandering to the window above the sink. The front yard was empty except for a red wheelbarrow and a few chickens pecking in the dirt. The first rays of sunlight made the dark sky glow orange. Miriam had made good on her plan to do the morning chores with Gideon, and Naomi could only imagine how that was going.

She flipped over the bacon in the pan, then glanced outside again. Grease sizzled and popped as she stood on her tiptoes and craned her neck to see past the farmyard, toward the goat shed.

"Hey, is something burning?" Benjamin asked from the doorway.

Naomi spun around. "What are you doing here?"

"Getting my breakfast. What else?" Benjamin leaned against the doorjamb and flashed a mischievous grin. "Why? What are you hiding?"

"Nothing. And aren't you supposed to be doing your morning chores?"

"Just finished." Benjamin sauntered across the kitchen and peered out the window in the same direction that Naomi had been looking. "Huh," he said, then turned to her. "It's almost as if you were trying to spy on Gideon."

Naomi pointed her spatula at him. "*Vell*, I wasn't. You can't see the goat shed from here."

"I didn't say you *were* spying. I said you were *trying* to. Unsuccessfully, obviously."

Naomi waved the spatula at her brother. "That's *lecherich*."

"Is it ridiculous?" Benjamin leaned his back against the butcher-block counter and raised his eyebrows. "Because it seems like you're pretty distracted. Which reminds me, you better check on those biscuits. They still smell like they're burning."

Naomi gasped and threw down the spatula. "*You* distracted me!"

Benjamin chuckled. "I don't think it was me." He braced his palms on the counter and lifted himself up to sit on top of it.

Naomi flung open the oven door, waved away the smoke, grabbed a pot holder, and pulled out the tray. Benjamin coughed dramatically.

"It's not that bad," Naomi said as she slammed the oven door closed before more smoke could escape.

Benjamin smiled. "Not as bad as your crush on Gideon."

Naomi dropped the tray on top of the range, turned to glare at Benjamin, and sputtered for a moment before she yelled at him to get off the counter.

Benjamin did not move. Instead, he began swinging his legs. His heels thumped against the wooden cabinets beneath the counter.

"I'm giving you the burnt biscuits and saving the rest for us," Naomi muttered.

"For Gideon, you mean."

Naomi clicked off the dial on the back of the propane-powered range.

A few beats passed. Naomi refused to look at Benjamin. Instead, she moved the bacon off the burner, then began to transfer the biscuits to a basket lined with a red-checkered cloth.

Benjamin's feet stopped swinging. "Hey, I was just joking. It's *oll recht* if you like him."

"I don't like him."

"You've never been a good liar. It's one of your best qualities."

"I'm not giving you an opportunity to tell me I'm wrong."

Benjamin sighed. "Look, I get it. I didn't want anyone to know that I had a crush on Emma for, *vell*, my whole life. I thought everyone would say she was out of my league. The thing about siblings is, they don't hold back when it comes to that kind of stuff."

"No, they don't." Naomi waited for Benjamin to say more but he looked as if he were trying to figure out how to respond. "So, is that why you're here? To tell me I'm being foolish?" Naomi narrowed her eyes and pointed a finger at him. "*If* I was sweet on Gideon. Which I'm not."

"Let's say you are, just in theory. So, if you *were* sweet on him, I guess I'd understand."

Naomi's eyes narrowed more. "You would?"

Benjamin shrugged. "Sure. Why not?"

"*Ach*, I think this family could come up with about a hundred reasons why not."

"*Vell*, I didn't say I wouldn't worry. I'd understand it a lot more than Miriam would, but I'd also worry that you might be jumping into things with someone we don't really know."

"You're putting the cart before the horse, Benjamin. I just told you I'm not sweet on Gideon." Naomi felt a twinge of guilt. Was she lying? Emotions were confusing things. Maybe it wasn't a complete lie. More of a misdirection. Regardless, she could not afford to let the truth out. Benjamin might tell Leah, since they were so close, then she might mention it to someone else—with the best intentions—but it would spread from there and then Naomi would never live it down. If she couldn't stop her feelings for Gideon, then she would have to keep them a complete secret. It was too early to know what she was really feeling, anyway. She barely knew him. Even if she did feel drawn to those guarded eyes and strong arms, his mysterious way of watching her without speaking and—

"Naomi, are you thinking of him right now?"

Naomi jumped. "What? Of course not. That's ridiculous."

"*Vell*, you've got that dreamy look in your eyes—"

"Can't you all let me move on? Just because I got it wrong before—"

"A couple times before."

"Fine." Naomi glared at Benjamin. "A couple times before."

"And you always got that same look when you were thinking about those suitors."

"I can learn lessons, Benji."

"I know you can." Benjamin crinkled his forehead. "But have you?"

Naomi could see the genuine concern in his eyes, but waved him off. "I'm fine. You don't have to be so protective."

"I'm your brother. I just want to make sure you're *oll recht*."

"I'm fine. I'm great."

"So great that you burned the biscuits because you were so busy looking for Gideon?"

Naomi threw up her hands. "Who knows what Miriam's saying to him right now!"

Benjamin's eyebrows shot up. "Aha! So, you admit it."

Naomi groaned, grabbed the basket of biscuits, and swept past Benjamin to carry it to the kitchen table. “Stop talking and eat. We’ve got the work frolic later, remember?” Viola Esch’s roof had been leaking, so Edna Yoder, the bishop’s wife, had organized for some of the men in the district to repair it.

Naomi heard the front door open and slam shut, followed by the sound of boots thumping against the floor as someone pulled them off their feet.

“Now you can ask Miriam all about her conversation with Gideon,” Benjamin whispered.

“Don’t you dare say a word,” Naomi said.

“Say a word about what?” Miriam asked as she padded into the kitchen in her sock feet.

“Nothing. We better hurry or we’ll be late.”

“Benjamin, get off the counter,” Miriam said. “Naomi’s right, we need to get going. You’re not going to make us late again.”

“But that’s my best quality.” Benjamin grinned as he dropped to the floor with a heavy thud. “Otherwise, you wouldn’t appreciate being on time.”

Miriam rolled her eyes, but couldn’t hide a slight smile.

Naomi adjusted the cloth covering the biscuits as she considered how to ask Miriam about her time with Gideon. “So,” she said after a few beats. “What did Gideon have to say?”

The hint of a smile on Miriam’s face fell into a frown. “Not much.” She shook her head as she grabbed a clean apron and tied it around her waist. “He’s too quiet.”

“There’s nothing wrong with being shy.”

Miriam glanced up at Naomi with a sharp expression before looking down to smooth her apron. “Unless he’s hiding something. There could be a reason he doesn’t talk.”

"You need to make sure he is who he says he is," Amanda said from the doorway.

"You've finished all the work in the production shed for the day?" Miriam asked.

"Of course. I'm ready to go to Viola's."

"You know, I hadn't thought of that," Benjamin said.

"Of what?" Naomi asked.

"That Gideon could be hiding his true identity."

"This isn't an *Englisch* spy movie, Benjamin."

Benjamin nodded toward Amanda. "She brought it up because it happened to her. It's possible."

"*Vell*, anything is *possible*!" Naomi crossed her arms. "But that doesn't mean it's *realistic*."

"Hold on," Amanda said. "David didn't hide his identity. Not exactly. We just didn't admit who we were when we were pen pals. It was…a special circumstance."

"Then why did you bring it up?"

"I didn't bring up David. I just pointed out that we don't know Gideon."

"I cannot believe that you're giving me a hard time right now, when you had a secret pen pal who you fell in love with! And what about Leah? We didn't know John when he moved into the extra room with his baby!"

"Bishop Amos knew John, so that was different," Miriam said as she turned to the skillet. "You left the bacon."

"Because I was too distracted by all of you saying outlandish things to get it on the table."

"We don't have time to eat at the table, anyway," Miriam said. "Put a couple slices of bacon in each of the biscuits and we'll take them as sandwiches to go. John has to lead the work frolic. He can't be late." John had built houses before marrying Leah, so he had experience in construction.

"Viola knows Gideon," Naomi said as she grabbed a knife from a drawer. "So it's no different than with John."

"Of course it's different," Amanda said. "Viola didn't know Gideon until this week. She just met him and wants to help."

"Or meddle," Miriam added.

"He could be anyone," Benjamin said.

Naomi looked up to glare at him but saw he was smiling. He winked and she shook her head at him.

"Benjamin, be serious," Miriam said. "This isn't a joke. We need to make sure that Naomi is..."

Naomi turned her attention to Miriam. "Is what, Miriam?"

"Is making good choices."

"I'm not a *kind*! I cannot believe you all! There's nothing wrong with being sweet on someone!"

"There is if it's with the wrong man," Miriam said.

"Wait." Amanda straightened up. "Are you saying you're sweet on Gideon?"

"*Nee*! Of course not! I'm talking theoretically!"

Benjamin bit his lip to keep from laughing. "Right. Theoretically."

The front door opened and everyone froze.

"Not a word!" Naomi hissed at Benjamin.

"Hey, I'm on your side," he whispered, then motioned toward their sisters. "They're the ones you have to worry about."

Naomi's pulse sped up as footsteps echoed down the hallway. She sifted through her mind for the perfect thing to say as she waited. But as soon as Gideon appeared in the doorway, all thoughts flew from her head and all she could think about were his brooding blue eyes.

He took off his straw hat as he stood in the threshold. "I,

uh, went ahead and hitched up the buggy." He began to turn his hat in his hands. "Hope that's *oll recht*."

Benjamin grinned. "You bet that's *oll recht*. Saved me the trouble." He gave Miriam a pointed look. "All that worrying over nothing. We're not going to be late."

"No thanks to you," she said before allowing a small smile. Miriam could never stay irritated at Benjamin for long. No one could.

Naomi was still trying to think of the perfect thing to say to Gideon. "Good morning!" she blurted out. "The weather is very nice today, ain't so?"

Gideon glanced out the window. "*Ya*. It's pretty *gut*."

Miriam and Amanda exchanged a look. Naomi knew that they knew she was struggling to make small talk, which only happened when she was sweet on a man. Why couldn't she do anything right? It was bad enough that her siblings suspected she was falling for yet another bad match, but now she looked silly in front of Gideon too. Why couldn't she be cleverer? What would Gideon think of her now?

As if that even mattered. She would barely get a chance to talk to him after this. Her sisters would make sure of that.

Gideon knew that the family had been talking about him. They had all stood in complete silence, staring at him, as he walked into the kitchen. He could only imagine what they had been saying, especially after his disastrous morning with Miriam. She had made sure that he did his chores alongside her and peppered him with questions the entire time. They weren't unreasonable ones, but he had felt tongue-tied nonetheless. It should not have been hard to tell her about his hometown and the church district in Holmes County where he grew up, but he just could not get the right words out. And, Miriam had not made it easy for him. She knew how to make him feel small with a single look. He was not sure that was intentional—she might make everyone feel that way—but it did not matter. He had blown his chance to make a good impression.

He had hoped that, by going the extra mile, he could prove that he was a *gut* enough worker to keep around. But that would not be enough if he could not gain her trust or respect. Why couldn't he get the right words out when he wanted to? Whenever someone asked him a question, he felt hot inside and his stomach churned and he knew everyone would assume he was a failure. It had become a self-fulfilling prophecy, because by answering questions so poorly, he proved that he *was* a failure.

"Hey, are you okay?" a voice whispered beside him.

Gideon looked over to see Naomi gazing up at him. He flinched. He must be frowning. It seemed like the harder he tried, the worse he did. "*Ya*, I'm *gut*."

She glanced over at the others, who were busy piling biscuits into to-go containers, then back to him. "You look upset."

"I was just thinking."

Naomi's expression shifted to interest. "About what?"

For an instant, Gideon was tempted to tell her. Her face looked so open and honest, her eyes so clear and genuine. But he could not risk exposing his feelings. "Nothing important."

"Oh."

Gideon could see what might have been a flicker of hurt pass over Naomi. He quickly told himself that it couldn't be helped, even though the sudden pang in his chest said otherwise. What if he trusted her? What if he made a connection here?

No. He would not put either of them in that situation. Besides, she might just be friendly by nature. He would not make assumptions. Better not to put her in an awkward situation when she was just trying to be nice.

"Get your breakfast, Gideon," Miriam said. Her no-nonsense tone snapped him out of his thoughts. Why did he feel like he was back in the schoolhouse, getting a scolding for breaking the rules, whenever she spoke to him? Because that was probably the way she saw him—an immature *bu* who broke the rules and ended up in trouble with the law for it. How could he ever live down his past when it followed him everywhere he went?

"Sure," he managed to say. "*Danki*."

"Naomi made them," Benjamin said as Gideon picked up a biscuit with a burnt spot on it.

Naomi glared at Benjamin and he grinned back at her. Gideon watched as Naomi's cheeks flushed pink. "I was… distracted," she murmured.

Benjamin raised his eyebrows at Naomi and she made a point to ignore him.

"Looks mighty *gut* to me," Gideon said. "I'll take two." He grabbed a biscuit that was even more burned than the one he had already taken and took a big bite. He nodded as he chewed, then swallowed. "*Danki*, Naomi. Biscuits are my favorite food." He did not mention that this particular biscuit was not his favorite. But he didn't care if Naomi was a good cook or not. He cared that she had worked hard to provide breakfast before a big day of work. She was probably distracted because she had so many chores to do. What really mattered was how kind she was. He would not forget that she treated him as if he were one of them, not an outsider trying to belong.

Footsteps banged down the stairwell, followed by the happy gurgling of a baby. "We're ready!" Leah shouted as she and Abby raced past the kitchen doorway, toward the front door. John followed close behind. "So am I!" Emma said as she swept by a moment later with Caleb in her arms. Katie trailed behind. "Hey, Gideon," she said as she skipped past him. Gideon smiled. At least some of the family seemed happy he was here.

A few minutes later, they were all piling into the back of the buggy, cramming onto the long bench seats that faced one another. Gideon wanted to be polite, so he stepped back and allowed the others to climb up in front of him. By the time it was his turn, the benches were full. He frowned and scratched his head. He was the odd man out. Again. Now what?

Naomi leaped up from the bench seat so fast that she banged her head. "We'll take the smaller buggy!" she said as she rubbed her scalp.

"I can—" Miriam started to say, but Naomi cut her off. "I'm already up." Naomi pushed past Benjamin and David, then hopped off the back of the buggy. She landed hard and Gideon instinctively reached out to grab her elbow and steady her. He heard her gasp and realized that he had crossed a line. But then he saw that she was smiling. Her eyes were bright as she gazed up at him. "You okay?" he asked.

"Oh, yes," she whispered, her eyes locked on his.

Gideon felt a flutter of joy. He had done something right. And it felt good to touch her warm, soft arm. It felt good to keep her safe.

And then he realized that it was too quiet. He looked past Naomi to see everyone in the buggy staring at him. His face heated up and he dropped Naomi's elbow. He had overstepped. He dropped his eyes, but could still feel everyone's gaze on him, hard and judgmental. Or maybe it just felt that way. He dared to glance around the buggy and noticed that

Benjamin had a knowing half smile. But Naomi's sisters were all stony-faced as they stared back at him.

Gideon cleared his throat. He was not doing a very good job of being inconspicuous.

"Come on," Naomi said. She tugged on his sleeve, then headed toward the barn. "Hurry up!" she called out over her shoulder.

Miriam elbowed Amanda, who then shouted, "I can take Gideon in the other buggy!"

"No need," Naomi shouted back, without turning around. "You're all settled in that buggy and ready to go. We shouldn't waste time, right, Miriam? You all get going and we'll catch up."

Gideon could hear Miriam sigh as he began jogging to catch up with Naomi. He was not going to miss a chance to be alone with her, especially when the alternative was to spend the drive in strained silence with one of her judgmental sisters. They clearly did not want him getting too cozy with Naomi, and he hoped that he wasn't causing trouble by going along with her suggestion. It made sense that they would be cautious. The family must be worried that Naomi would fall for the wrong fellow. She was the only single sister left besides Miriam, but Miriam could intimidate an unworthy suitor with one look, for certain sure.

Gideon bristled at the thought that Naomi's sisters didn't trust her to make her own decisions. She was clearly intelligent and goodhearted. Why give her such a hard time about a buggy ride? She was competent enough to discern for herself whether or not to give Gideon a chance.

Wait. *Give him a chance?* Naomi would not be sweet on a drifter with a criminal background. And even if she were—which was a ridiculous thought—a match between the two of them could never work. He would be going his own way in just a couple of weeks. And he would not allow his heart to get torn in two. Besides, even if he were able to stay, Naomi's family would never approve. He did not want to damage those relationships. He knew how important family was, since he had lost his. He would never come between Naomi and hers.

So, as he watched the rest of the family drive away in a cloud of dust and the crunch of buggy wheels on gravel, Gideon pushed away his desire for a connection. He had been alone this long and done just fine. Well, mostly fine.

His resolve weakened as soon as he looked over to Naomi. Her smile was so bright that it lit up her entire face. "Come on!" she said as she pushed open the big barn door with a slow creak. "We better get the buggy hitched up fast or we'll never hear the end of it."

Gideon gave a nervous laugh. He wanted to relax and enjoy a few moments with this fun-loving woman, but he was too worried that he might be causing strife between Naomi and her sisters. Plus, he was feeling too nervous. Which was odd. Why should he feel nervous around her? She was so open and accepting. But when he turned to look into her deep brown eyes, his stomach plunged to his toes. What was wrong with him?

The familiar earthy smells of animals met him as he followed Naomi inside the barn. A brown-and-white-speckled horse whinnied and stamped a hoof against the concrete floor.

"Hey there, Rocket," Naomi murmured as she reached out to pat the horse's neck. "Clyde used to be our only buggy horse, but the family has been growing so fast that we bought Rocket. And an extra buggy." She motioned toward the small two-seater buggy with an open top parked in the corner. She looked back at Gideon, then said, "It's a courting buggy."

Was she hinting? No, surely not. But she *was* staring up at him with those soft brown eyes. He was so caught off guard that he just kept staring back. What could he possibly say in response to that? The moment passed with agonizing slowness. He could hear the tick of his heart in this throat and the rustle of hay in Rocket's stall. After a few beats, Naomi dropped her eyes and adjusted her apron. "We got it because it was a *gut* deal. Not because..." She cleared her throat. "Miriam loves a bargain. They were selling it cheap because it was used and a little worn."

"*Recht*. Of course. That makes sense." What didn't make sense was that Naomi had been hinting about something more when it came to that buggy—and the two of them riding in it. Or had he just imagined that? She looked so embarrassed that he wanted to say something to make her laugh, to put her at ease. But, of course, he couldn't think of anything. He was not clever like that. He had always wanted to be funny, but it just wasn't something that came naturally. "A *gut* deal is a *gut* deal."

Naomi's eyes shot back up and her face brightened. "Exactly."

Then it occurred to Gideon that Naomi had not been giving a hint about wanting to court him. She had just been sheepish about asking him to ride in a courting buggy. It was the opposite of what he had suspected. She wanted him to know that she *wasn't* interested. That made a lot more sense. He would have to reassure her by keeping things distant and formal. Which was also best for him. It would be win-win.

He just wished the ache in his heart didn't say otherwise.

"I'll get Rocket hitched up real quick and we'll be on our way." Naomi headed toward the tack hanging from the wall.

"I've got this," Gideon said. He would keep his distance,

but he wouldn't let her do the work when he was there to do it for her.

"Oh." Naomi flashed a brilliant smile. "Okay."

It felt good to step in and take over the job. But then he began to feel awkward. He didn't want her to see him fumble or make a mistake. But then, thankfully, she headed toward the stall. "I'll get Rocket while you get the tack," she said. It was as if she had read his mind. Or maybe she felt as awkward as he did, just standing there, watching him work.

Rocket snorted as she led him toward the buggy. "Easy now," she murmured. "Gideon's a *gut* man. You'll like him."

Did she really think that about him? Was she willing to set aside any prejudice and judge him on his actions in the present? Her words repeated in his head as he began buckling the harness. The leather creaked and the metal buckle jangled. He felt like he should say something. "*Danki*."

"For what?" Naomi asked. She reached over to help him with the lead.

"Oh, um, saying that about me, I guess."

Naomi laughed, the sound as light and carefree as a bell. "*Vell*, it's true, ain't so?" Her hand slipped around Rocket's neck to hand Gideon the lead. His fingers brushed against hers as he took it from her grasp. Her skin was so soft and warm. He wished he could tighten his hand around hers and hold her, just for a moment. He wanted that connection, even though he knew he should resist it.

Naomi's eyes met his from across Rocket's back. Their hands lingered and Gideon felt the moment pulse through him. Sunlight streamed in through the cracks in the rustic, unpainted walls, highlighting her eyelashes and the dust motes in the air around her.

"Ain't so?" Naomi repeated.

"What?"

"That you're a *gut* man."

"Oh." Gideon swallowed hard. "I hope so. I try to be. But…"

"But what?"

Gideon remembered that his fingers were still touching hers and pulled them back. He tried to focus on fastening the lead. "*Vell*, I've made mistakes. And I'm not where I want to be in life."

"We all make mistakes," Naomi said.

Gideon laughed. He kept his eyes on the leather harness. "Some are worse than others."

Naomi watched him for a moment. "What do you mean that you're not where you want to be? Where do you want to be?"

"I want to be well off enough to have my own farm, get married, and have my own family. I want to be…" He almost said *loved*. He almost said that he wanted to belong. It was too easy to fall into conversation with Naomi and reveal more than he should. He pushed aside matters of the heart and went back to the practical and obvious. "It takes money to do that. And I've not managed to get much yet."

Naomi tilted her head as she stared up at him. Her fingers moved through Rocket's mane automatically, as if it were second nature, while her mind was elsewhere. "But you're Amish. You don't need money to be somebody. That's an *Englisch* way of thinking."

Gideon sighed. She made it sound so simple. And it would be for her. She owned a big, prosperous farm. "We say that, but we don't always mean it."

Her chin rose slightly and her eyes flashed. "Well, I mean it."

Gideon couldn't help but smile. "I know you do." She had a good heart. It would get her in trouble, if she weren't careful. No wonder her family was worried that she might fall for the wrong man. "But even so, it doesn't solve the practical problem. I can't support a *frau* without a *gut* steady income. And I've had a string of bad luck—"

"Amish don't believe in bad luck either. Everything that happens is *Gott*'s will."

"I like that idea."

"It's not an idea. It's the truth."

Gideon nodded slowly. "Things haven't gone well for me..."

"Maybe you just can't see the end of the journey. If everything that has happened takes you to where you're supposed to go, *vell*, it will be worth it in the end."

Gideon felt an unexpected surge of confidence. She made it sound so straightforward. "You make it easier to believe," he murmured.

She bit her lip and stared into his eyes.

Why had he admitted that? Somehow, he had fallen into her optimism. She had given him a feeling that he had almost forgotten—that *Gott* walked with him and had a plan for him, despite his circumstances. He quickly turned his attention to buckling the last buckle. "We should get going," he said. He had crossed a line that would only lead to heartache, for both of them. If he could not resist their connection for his own sake, then he owed it to her to keep his distance.

Chapter Five

Naomi could not understand what had happened. Had she said the wrong thing? Had she been too forward? Gideon had seemed so open, so genuine in the barn as they hitched up the buggy together. And she had been sure that his hand had lingered on hers for longer than expected when she passed him the lead. That moment had sent a ripple of excitement through her.

Until she settled onto the bench seat next to him, and the buggy took off in a jerk and rattled across the gravel driveway. Gideon had not spoken since then. Naomi adjusted the reins in her hands and glanced over at him. He was staring straight ahead, his jaw set, his eyes guarded. What had she done wrong? Maybe he was irritated that she was driving instead of him. Some men liked to be the ones to drive. But Gideon didn't seem like the type to get hung up on a silly detail like that. Besides, Rocket didn't like it when strangers drove, so it just made sense for her to be the one behind the reins.

Her sisters were always telling her that she got caught up in her feelings. Perhaps she wasn't being reasonable. Naomi watched the long golden stalks of wheat wave in the field alongside the road as she searched for the right words to say. Maybe he just needed a little nudge. He could be feeling shy. After all, they had practically held hands. Maybe he was worried that *he* had been too forward!

Naomi cleared her throat. "It's a *gut* crop of wheat this year." She cringed as soon as she said it. Wheat was not a romantic subject. It was not even an interesting subject.

Gideon nodded politely, but said nothing.

"I hear there's going to be a big mud sale in the Little Creek district this Saturday. I've been thinking about going. But I don't like..." Naomi stopped.

Gideon turned his head to look at her. "You don't like what?" His brow crinkled in a way that made him seem like he was genuinely interested in what she had to say.

"*Ach, vell...*" She shifted in her seat. "I was just going to say that I don't like going alone." Naomi swallowed hard and waited, keeping her eyes on the road ahead. Had she crossed a line? Miriam would certainly say so. But what did Miriam know?

"Oh." Gideon didn't say anything for a moment. He looked back at the road and rubbed the back of his neck. "I guess I don't like going alone to things like that either."

Naomi's stomach churned with happy butterflies. He was hinting back to her, wasn't he? She tried to stop a smile from taking over her face. She didn't want to look too goofy. She waited for him to ask her to go with him as her heart hammered in her chest. Suddenly, the sky seemed a brighter blue, the grass a more vibrant green, and the birds in the fields were singing more loudly.

Gideon looked out over the fields. His eyes followed an *Englisch* pickup truck throwing up dust along a dirt side road. "But it doesn't matter because I'll be at Stoneybrook Farm all day Saturday. There'll be plenty of work to do."

Naomi felt herself deflate like a balloon. Was he rejecting her? She had been so sure of their connection. Had he not understood what she was hinting at? That could explain everything. He probably did not want to overstep. After all, Miriam could be quite a deterrent. She just needed to ask him outright. Then he would surely say yes. Miriam would have a fit if she found out Naomi had been that forward, but she would just have to get over it.

Naomi glanced over at Gideon as she tried to arrange the words in her head. He looked distant, on edge. That was not the expression of a man hoping to take a woman out to a mud sale.

Naomi focused her eyes back on the road and tightened her grip on the reins. Was she reading him wrong? Oh, how she hoped so! But there was no way she could breach the silence now. Not when he looked like he wanted nothing to do with her.

Shame flared through her as her face heated up. Had she just thrown herself at a man who was utterly disinterested? What about that connection she had felt in the barn? It was all too confusing.

She spent the rest of the buggy ride in silence, trying to make sense of the emotions swirling through her. Gideon did not say another word until Viola's farmhouse came into view. A dog lying on the front porch scrambled to his feet and began to bark. "It's just us, Blue!" Naomi shouted to the old hound. He wagged his tail slowly, and settled back onto the worn wooden floorboards.

The buggy rumbled into Viola's yard to park on the grass alongside a handful of other buggies.

"*Danki* for the ride," Gideon murmured before hopping down and heading toward the group of men standing beside the house with tools in their hands. They looked like Gideon in their straw work hats, solid blue shirts, black suspenders, and black broad fall pants, but something was different about him. Something that she couldn't quite put into words, yet felt deep inside.

Naomi watched Gideon walking across the yard. He was so handsome and lost-looking that he made her heart ache. And the distance he was putting between them only made her want to draw closer to him. She felt dizzy with the need to understand him, to be reassured by him.

"Try not to be so obvious, Naomi."

Naomi flinched. Benjamin was standing beside the buggy, giving her a sly look. He leaned his elbows onto the window frame and grinned. "Or at least don't be so obvious in front of anyone else."

"I'm not being obvious."

"Uh-huh. Okay."

"Shouldn't you be over there with the men?" Naomi raised her chin a fraction. "You've got your own business to get to, ain't so? So why don't you let me mind mine, *oll recht*?"

Benjamin sighed. "I was just joking." He glanced over to the group of men. John was already scrambling up a tall ladder, toward the roof.

"I know, but I'm getting tired of it."

"Sorry." Benjamin pushed away from the buggy. "I should have just told you outright to be careful. It's clear as day how you feel about Gideon."

"You're not so *gut* at reading people, you know."

Benjamin raised his eyebrows.

"Okay. Maybe it is obvious. Just don't tell anybody, especially Miriam."

"I won't have to if you don't hide it better."

Naomi threw open the buggy door and slid to the ground. "Fine. And not that it's any of your business, but Gideon isn't interested anyway. So you don't have to worry."

Benjamin frowned. "You sure about that?"

Naomi shrugged, then patted Rocket on the neck. She wasn't sure about anything at this point—except for her own feelings for Gideon.

"Hey, Benji!" John shouted from the roof. "Can you grab my other hammer from the back of the buggy?"

Benjamin jogged away and Naomi found herself staring at Gideon again. He looked so strong and competent as he hammered away at the roof, one nail held between his lips, another between two fingers as he slammed the hammer down. He took the nail from his lips held it in place, then hammered it into a shingle with two good strikes. Gideon glanced up and his eyes met Naomi's. She jerked her gaze from his. When she dared to peek, he was looking at her. She smiled and he smiled back. Her butterflies returned.

She was not giving up on this man. The least she could do was get to know him better. He was too mysterious not to try.

Gideon had not done a very good job of maintaining his distance from Naomi. He had nearly asked her to go to the mud sale with him. And she had caught him looking at her from the rooftop. He had even smiled back at her. It was all he could do not to run straight to her and tell her how much he wanted to step out with her.

This had to stop.

It had been all he had thought about that day. He sighed, hit the last nail, and set down the hammer.

John paused on the ladder. "You coming?"

"Huh? Uh, yeah."

"Leah baked her famous shoofly pie. It's sure to be *gut*."

Gideon managed to nod. "Can't beat that."

"Sure can't." John disappeared down the ladder.

Gideon took a deep breath and let it out slowly. He had to go face the crowd now. Thankfully it wasn't a huge work frolic, but it was big enough. There were sure to be questions. Fortunately, the men hadn't talked too much while they worked. But now that the work was finished, everyone would expect him to make small talk. He would not know what to say, which would make them suspicious. They would have already heard about his past through the Amish grapevine, so they would be looking for a reason to judge him. And, shy as he was, he would be awkward enough to give them one.

"Pie's getting cold!" John shouted from the ground.

"Yep. On my way." Gideon sighed again, then padded down the ladder and followed the men into Viola's house. The smell of brown sugar and fresh-baked bread met him in the doorway along with the low murmur of cheerful voices. He wiped his boots on the doormat, then walked slowly toward the noise.

"Gideon!" Naomi slipped past a woman holding a basket of rolls to meet Gideon at the kitchen door.

He felt a whoosh of relief and could not stop himself from smiling. "Hey."

Naomi's face lit up as she returned his smile. "Hey."

"It's pretty crowded in there." Her expression faltered for an instant. "I, uh, hope you don't mind but I went ahead and fixed you a plate."

"*Nee*, I don't mind." Gideon wanted to tell her how much he appreciated that she was looking out for him. Somehow, she had known that he could not face going in there, among all the talkative strangers. But he didn't know how to explain how thankful he was to be understood by her, so he said nothing. She peered up at him for an awkward moment, then looked away. "The table's full. See if you can find a spot in the living room."

Gideon nodded.

A skinny woman strode through the crowded kitchen,

pushed past Naomi, and stared at Gideon. “Ah, there you are.” She looked to be in her early sixties, judging by her gray hair and the frown lines on her forehead, but she moved like a much younger woman. “I’ve been waiting to talk to you.”

Naomi slid closer to Gideon. “*Vell*, he was just about to eat, so it’ll have to wait. Besides, I need help with my potato salad. Something doesn’t seem right. Maybe you can taste it and see what it needs?”

The elderly woman gave a curt nod. “You never can get the seasoning right. *Gut* thing you asked me. I’ll take care of it.” She turned on her heels and marched away.

“Whew.” Naomi stifled a giggle as she shook her head. “That was close.”

Gideon frowned. “Should I be worried?” He wanted to make a joke asking how a little old lady could be any danger, but knew he wasn’t clever enough, so he said nothing.

Naomi glanced behind her, then leaned closer and lowered her voice. “That’s Lovina Zook. She means well.” Naomi’s brow crinkled. “*Vell*, I think she means well… Never mind. Just try to avoid her. Otherwise, she’ll corner you and put you on the spot in front of everybody. It’s just the way she is.”

“Avoid Lovina. Got it.” He tried to sound casual and nonchalant, but his mind was racing. Lovina could humiliate him in front of the entire work frolic.

“I have to get back to serving.” Naomi started to turn away, then looked back at him. Her big brown eyes seemed so soft and trusting. “But maybe I’ll see you later.”

“I hope so.” He had not meant to say it. But she made him feel so seen and understood. She had known that Lovina would put him in an awkward situation and she had protected him. Gideon laughed at the thought.

“What’s so funny?”

"I was just thinking about how you had to protect me from a little old woman."

Naomi laughed. "Everyone needs protecting from Lovina. You'll understand once you get to know her."

"Oh, I think I understand already." He glanced over to where Lovina was sampling Naomi's potato salad. She frowned and shook her head as she chewed, then reached for a spice jar.

"I'll never hear the end of it about that potato salad," Naomi said. "Which was perfect, by the way."

"I'm sure it was."

"Lovina and I have always disagreed about how much apple cider vinegar and celery seed it needs."

Gideon shifted the plate in his hand so that he could pick up the fork. He took a big bite of potato salad, chewed, and swallowed. "Tastes just right to me."

Naomi gave a triumphant nod. "Exactly."

"Hey, Naomi, we're running low on lemonade," Miriam said loudly enough for her voice to carry across the noisy kitchen. "*Kumme* make some more."

"Gotta go."

As Gideon watched Naomi disappear into the crowd, all he could think about was how much he hoped that they could spend more time together soon. Then he remembered that he was hovering awkwardly in the kitchen doorway and needed to find a seat. He wandered into the living room, which was already full of men who couldn't fit at the table. A few glanced up, but most of them didn't notice him. They were too busy eating and chatting with one another. He did not know any of them.

The room was neat and tidy, just as he expected Viola's home would be. The plain space had few furnishings, just a propane lampstand and a quilt rack with a colorful quilt draped across it, in addition to the dark green sofa and chairs. Gideon settled onto a glider, the only free chair left in the room, and tried to balance his plate on his lap. But when he moved, the glider slid forward and his roll tumbled off his plate and hit the floor. Gideon flinched and grabbed the roll as quickly as he could. He hoped no one had noticed.

He caught snippets of conversation while he ate, mostly about the price of corn and a storm that had caused some damage to the crops on the other side of Lancaster County. One of the men asked him where he was from and what corn was selling for in Holmes County, but Gideon didn't have much to say, so no one asked him any more questions after that. He wished he could be more talkative, but that just wasn't his way. He was a better listener. And, as he listened to the conversations on either side of him, he started to get a pretty good picture of the church district and the latest news. It sounded like a tight-knit community with lots of prosperous farms.

Tight-knit communities could be hard to break into. But maybe he could enjoy his time here, as long as it lasted. Everyone had been pretty welcoming, so far. They weren't pushing him to talk, anyway. And they weren't asking too many questions. Maybe news hadn't traveled that fast on the Amish grapevine yet. Or maybe they just didn't care about the gossip.

A couple of men were speaking in low voices while looking over at him, but Gideon told himself that it didn't mean anything. He wanted to give them the benefit of the doubt. He was just starting to let his guard down when Lovina strode into the room with a tray full of mugs. "Ah, there you are." She nodded toward Gideon, then set the tray down on the coffee table. Instead of leaving, she stood with her hands on her hips, surveying the room. She was not going to let him remain anonymous.

The men began to grab mugs of coffee from the tray and Gideon imitated them. He did not want to stand out. He took a big sip, and burned his tongue. He did not mind that the coffee was too hot, because it was also strong and black, just like it was at every work frolic. That felt comforting somehow. He liked things to be familiar.

Lovina strode across the room to where Gideon sat. "Finally," she said. "I've got a chance to speak to you."

Gideon nodded. He was not sure what she expected him to say.

"You should know that our church district is different from what you're used to."

Gideon stared at her. He could tell by her tone and the way she peered down the end of her nose at him that this was not going to go well.

"We keep to the *ordnung* around here."

The low murmur of conversation died down as everyone in the room turned their attention to him and Lovina.

"Do you understand?"

Gideon's collar felt too tight, his face too hot. He had already repented. He wasn't going to accept a public shaming without pushing back. "I'm not sure that I do. Bishop Amos has welcomed me to the Bluebird Hills church district. He's the one who found me a job and a place to stay with a *gut* family."

Lovina's lips tightened as she studied him. Gideon realized that she had not expected him to stand up for himself. "*Vell*," she said after a moment, "Viola would know if anything goes missing from her house. I just thought you should know that. We all look out for each other here."

There was a sharp intake of breath from one of the men

on the sofa. Another man cleared his throat. Gideon could feel the sudden shift in the room. Everyone was waiting to hear what he would say. But how could he respond to that? He didn't want to be too harsh with an elderly woman. She might have reason to be suspicious, though nothing would give her the excuse to humiliate him like this.

He was thinking through his next words when he heard a cane tapping on the hardwood floor. The rhythmic noise grew louder in the hushed room, until Viola appeared in the doorway. "*Ah*, *gut*," she announced with gusto. "You've all gotten a chance to meet this fine young *mann*. I've been too busy to find you until now." She hobbled into the living room and shooed the man in the closest chair from him. The man stood up fast and stepped aside. Viola nodded to Gideon and lowered herself into the vacated chair with a heavy sigh. "Feels *gut* to sit down. Not as young as I used to be." She looked across the room and gave Lovina a pointed look. "But that's not a bad thing. Wisdom comes with age. Ain't so, Lovina?"

"Hmm," Lovina murmured, lips still tight.

"And I've got a good quarter of a century on you," Viola said. "So that makes me older *and* wiser, ain't so?"

A few of the men glanced at one another. One gray-haired man with an ample midsection was trying to suppress a smile. Gideon realized that Viola was much older than she seemed, even if she did need a cane to get around. In fact, he suspected that the cane was more for show than necessity. He had noticed that she liked to wave it around or hit the floor with it to make a point.

"So," Viola continued, "I'm sure that in your wisdom—even if it is less than mine—you have had the *gut* sense to welcome this young man into our church district."

"I am giving him just the right welcome."

"I'm sure you are," Viola said.

Lovina bristled but managed a syrupy smile. "*Danki*. I am *gut* at knowing what needs to be said."

"*Vell*, this is my house, so I will say what needs to be said. But *danki*, Lovina, for your...thoughtfulness." Viola turned to the rest of the room. "Now it's time you all met Gideon. I hope you've all introduced yourselves already." Viola gave pointed looks to the men sitting on the sofa and chairs. A few nodded, but most looked down at their plates. "Be sure that you do." Viola gave them a look that would have made the biggest man feel like a chastised schoolboy. "Now, it's time to introduce yourself, Gideon. I can see that you've been sitting over there alone. Have you said a word to anyone throughout the entire meal?"

Gideon frowned. "Uh, sure. Yeah, I said something."

"Not enough, I'm sure." She turned to look at the men in the room. "He's shy. Don't let it keep you from getting to know him. He's a *gut* man. You may have heard otherwise." Viola glared at Lovina. Someone coughed and another man shuffled his boots on the hardwood floor. After a pause, Viola continued, "Yes, he got into a little trouble with the *Englisch*. They dealt with it in the *Englisch* way. We would have done things differently. He stole food, which never should have happened. It never should have happened because his church district should have been helping him. We would never let it come to that here in Bluebird Hills, would we, Lovina?"

Lovina blinked a few times.

"*Gut*. I'm glad we agree."

Gideon wanted to sink into the floor. It was bad enough that she just told everyone that he had been arrested for stealing. But somehow, it felt even more humiliating that he had been poor enough to have to steal.

"Now, we're going to let that all be in the past, ain't so?" When no one responded, Viola thumped the floor with her cane to emphasize her words. "Ain't so? Because he's repented. So we're not going to hold it against him."

They might not hold the theft against him, but Gideon was more afraid that they would hold the poverty against him. He had seen it before, in the judgmental stares and quiet whispers accusing him of being lazy, of lacking what it takes to be Amish. How could he try so hard, and everything still slip through his fingers like water through a sieve? It seemed inconceivable, but there was always another unexpected expense, another disappointment, another job that had to let him go because they needed to lay off the most recent hire.

"Viola's right."

Gideon's attention shot to the living room door. Naomi stood in the threshold with her arms crossed, her expression more serious than he'd ever seen. Instead of sparkling with lighthearted joy, her eyes flashed with determination. "Gideon's a *gut* hard worker. He's a *gut* man."

A warm wave washed over Gideon. Naomi was there, standing up for him. It was one thing for Viola to stand up for him—and he really appreciated it—but she had a lot less to lose than Naomi did. She was pushing back against her own family to make such a public announcement on his behalf. There would surely be blowback. At the very least, everyone would think they were sweet on each other. How could he protect her reputation while showing her how much he appreciated her? This relationship was getting even more complicated.

Nee. There was no relationship. He was getting way ahead of himself. He needed to slow down and focus. But all he could think about in that moment was how strong Naomi looked, her eyes bright with emotion, her cheeks flushed, and her chin raised. She was a force to be reckoned with and he loved her for it.

He did not love her. Not in that way. He was not *in* love with her. He barely knew her. But he could love her as a person, as a friend, as someone he admired and respected. What he could not do is let him fall *in* love with her. Those were two very different things. And he was strong enough to put up the walls that needed to stay between them—for both of their sakes. He just had to ignore the rush of joy he felt whenever they were together.

Chapter Six

Naomi's heart pounded in her throat. Had she said too much or too little? She studied Gideon's expression. He was a hard man to read, but she was sure that she caught a glint of appreciation in his eyes. It was just like the Amish romance novels, where the plucky heroine stands up for the mysterious stranger. Well, to be honest, it was usually the hero who stood up for the heroine. But Gideon had needed her. Maybe next time he could rescue her. The problem was, she just didn't need rescuing very often. But maybe something would go wrong and he could swoop in to save her.

But for now, Naomi needed to enjoy the moment. She had just made a very romantic overture toward the man she was falling for—and she had done it in front of everyone. Maybe she should feel a little sheepish. After all, she had just made it pretty obvious that she was sweet on Gideon. But she did not feel sheepish. Not one bit. She felt a newfound strength coursing through her veins. Love had won today.

Okay, not love exactly. They were not even courting. But she certainly had strong feelings for him. And she could see that developing into love. Fast. Or maybe it was already an early kind of love. Did she believe in love at first sight? Gideon had certainly had a huge impact on her from the moment she laid eyes on him. Miriam would say that Naomi was just too caught up in her emotions and that she needed to come back down to earth.

Maybe it was best not to analyze it too much. She would just feel what she felt and let things happen… And right now, she felt giddy as Gideon looked at her from across the room. His eyes were steady, his expression open. They were connecting again. She was sure of it.

"Naomi, stop hovering and sit down," Viola said. "You're making me nervous."

Naomi had forgotten that she was standing in the doorway, staring at Gideon. She had forgotten that anyone else in the house existed except for him. Suddenly, the noise returned to the room, along with the scent of black coffee, and the distant sound of dishes clanging in the kitchen sink across the hallway.

All the seats were taken and Gideon stood up to offer her his chair. Just when Naomi did not think her heart could beat any faster, it did. This was surely a sign that he was falling for her too.

Or maybe he was just being polite. Maybe the entire room was cringing at her outburst for Gideon.

No. She would not let her mind go to those places. She would stay steady and strong. She knew these feelings were real.

"Ah, there you are," Miriam's voice said from behind her. "I need help with the dishes."

Naomi sighed. "Of course you do."

Miriam shot her a look, followed by an almost imperceptible shake of her head. Naomi knew that reaction well. Miriam wanted to be sure that Naomi followed the rules in front of everyone else. Naomi sighed again. "I'm coming."

Gideon hesitated, then nodded to Naomi and sank back into his chair. She smiled at him, perhaps too obviously, before following Miriam back to the kitchen. The room bustled with activity and the low hum of conversation. Miriam noticed the basket on the table and pointed. "Naomi, you didn't take the cinnamon rolls to the men."

"*Ach*, I forgot."

"Then what were you doing in there?"

Naomi shrugged. "I'll take them now." She reached for the basket but Miriam swooped in and grabbed it first. She passed the basket to Amanda, who happened to be strolling past them at that moment.

"Amanda can take it. Right, Amanda?"

"Uh, sure. But wasn't Naomi—"

"I need Naomi's help with the dishes," Miriam interrupted.

"Ohhh, right. Okay. Sure." Amanda grabbed the basket and headed across the hall.

Naomi rolled her eyes. "You're not being very subtle, Miriam."

"And neither are you. We'll talk later. For now, let's not make a scene."

"I'm not the one making a scene. I was about to quietly drink a cup of coffee with Gideon, remember? Almost everyone else is taking a coffee break, you know."

"Leah and Emma are taking care of Caleb and Abby. I think Katie's helping them."

"And everyone else?"

Edna Yoder set the last dish onto the drying rack, rung out the dishrag, and spread it out to dry. The rest of the women were already standing in clusters talking, pouring cups of coffee, and eating shoofly pie.

"Someone needs to dry the dishes."

"After I have my coffee."

Miriam pinched the bridge of her nose. "Naomi, please don't make this difficult."

"I'm not the one making anything difficult."

Miriam sighed and lowered her hand. "What do I have to do to make you see reality?"

"I can't believe you just said that." Naomi knew what Miriam thought of her, but this was going too far. "I am perfectly grounded in reality, thank you very much."

"You know what I mean."

"*Nee*, I do not. What don't you explain it to me?"

A few faces turned to look at Miriam and Naomi. Miriam frowned and leaned closer to Naomi. "Fine. You win for now," she said in a whisper. "We'll talk about this later."

"It isn't about winning, Miriam."

"You're right. It's not about winning. It's about losing. And you have everything to lose, Naomi."

Miriam's words pounded inside Naomi's mind after that. She tried to enjoy her coffee while she listened to the latest news, but her gaze kept sliding to the door. All she could think about was Gideon in the room across the hall, alone among strangers. If only they could sit side by side without anyone jumping to silly conclusions.

After a tense buggy ride home—and this time Miriam made sure that Naomi rode with her, while Benjamin and Gideon took the smaller buggy back—Miriam let Naomi know exactly what she thought. "You can control your feelings, you know," she said.

Naomi had barely slid out of the buggy when the lecture began. She hurried across the farmyard, Miriam close on her heels. The chickens scattered and Belinda the goose honked as they strode past. "You can control your actions, but not your feelings," Naomi said.

"You know what I mean." Miriam's legs were shorter and

she had to walk double-time to keep up with Naomi. Her breath was coming hard when they reached the front porch steps. Naomi bounded up them and Miriam jogged to keep up, her black athletic shoes thudding hard against the worn floorboards.

Naomi tore open the door and paused just long enough to announce over her shoulder, "And when you fall for someone, you can't stop that."

Miriam caught the screen door before it slammed in her face. "What are you saying? That you've already fallen for Gideon? See, this is exactly what I'm talking about."

Naomi realized that she had spoken without thinking. She was painting herself into a corner. If she told Miriam how she really felt, she would never hear the end of it. Worse, Miriam might try to separate her from Gideon. She might even send him away before his two weeks were up. "I didn't say that I had fallen for him. I said that you can't help it if you do. I was using the general *you*, not the *you* that means *me*." It wasn't a lie, exactly. She did believe that, as a general principle.

"So, you haven't fallen for Gideon?"

"*Vell*, that would be mighty quick, wouldn't it?" Naomi was proud of herself. She had been careful not to answer directly, but also not to lie.

"It certain sure would!"

"I'm not as flighty as you think I am, Miriam."

"Then prove it! Stop following him around like a lovesick puppy."

Naomi recoiled as if she had been slapped. "You can't mean that!"

Miriam frowned. "I'm sorry. I shouldn't have said that. But you are being a bit obvious, ain't so? Do you really want the entire church district to know how you feel?"

"Look, I don't know what you heard, but someone had to stand up to Lovina."

Miriam stiffened. "What?"

Naomi realized that she had just made a serious blunder. "*Ach*, never mind."

"*Nee*, not never mind. What did you do before I came into the room?" Miriam's brow creased as if she were deeply concerned. That was worse than if she had looked angry. "You know I'll hear about it sooner or later."

Miriam was right. Especially since Viola had been there. Soon, everyone would know. In fact, the only surprising thing was that Viola had not mentioned it to Miriam before they left the work frolic. Or that Lovina had not marched up to Miriam to complain about Naomi speaking out. Nobody but Viola stood up to Lovina, and there was a reason for that.

"Naomi."

The way Miriam looked at Naomi made her feel about three inches tall. She was so tired of feeling small and foolish around her sisters. What was so wrong with falling in love or dreaming about falling in love? "Someone had to defend Gideon from Lovina."

"It didn't have to be you. I'm sure Viola was doing a fine job without your help. She was there, right?"

"Ya."

"Then why put yourself out there like that? It's just asking for gossip."

"It was the right thing to do."

Miriam squeezed her eyes shut, exhaled, then opened her eyes. "I understand that. And I'm proud of you for always standing up for others. But maybe this isn't the time, especially when Viola is taking care of it. I know how much you want to find a *gut* husband. I worry that this could hurt your chances."

Naomi's immediate instinct was to say that she had already found a good candidate. But she knew better than to admit that outright. "If this hurts my chances with someone, then he would not have been a *gut* husband."

"Oh, Naomi. I can't protect you forever. You're just so naive."

"I am not naive! Maybe I'm the one who sees things the way they really are! You chased away your only suitor and I'm not going to make that same mistake. I believe that love can overcome anything."

A quiet mask overtook her sister's face. "I see." The words sounded distant and controlled.

"*Nee*, I didn't mean it like that—"

"We both know that you did." Miriam's voice was too calm. It made Naomi feel even worse than she already did. It would be easier if Miriam shouted or cried. Instead, she just seemed to disappear behind an impenetrable wall.

"I didn't. I'm sorry—"

Miriam gave a quick nod of her head. "I've got to see to the goats." And then she was gone with a swish of her purple skirt.

Naomi leaned against the wall and let out a long slow breath. She never should have said that. Miriam had broken off her courtship when their parents died because she insisted on putting the family first. But Naomi always wondered why Miriam couldn't do both. Wasn't there a way that she could have been with the man she loved *and* taken care of her siblings? Now, the man was long gone. Moved to Pinecraft, Florida, last she had heard.

Naomi had crossed a line that she knew better than to cross. Everyone knew not to bring up the subject of Miriam's lost love. Naomi would have to apologize, but she would wait until Miriam cooled down. And she would dread it until then, especially since she knew that she had been in the wrong. It just got her so riled up when Miriam acted as if love were silly and immature. Love was not silly and it was not immature. Love was real. It was what made life worth living.

Naomi heard the sound of voices on the front porch moving closer. She pushed away from the wall and braced herself. No one could know how she really felt. If she hid it well enough, then maybe Miriam and her other siblings would stop trying to keep them apart. And, just maybe, they would eventually realize that Gideon was a worthy suitor.

If he even wanted to be a suitor, that is. She did not intend to let love slip through her fingers. Even if it took a little bit of stealth.

Gideon tried to work beside Naomi as the family did the chores that evening, but she kept slipping away. It seemed like every time he looked for her, she was not nearby. He missed seeing her smile beside him as they milked the goats. He missed hearing her voice. Instead, the barn was filled with the whirr of the diesel milking machine, the bleating of goats, the click-clack of hooves, and the low murmur of voices as Benjamin and Leah chatted. Katie hummed as she skipped in and out of the goat shed, hauling buckets of milk to the production building. These were good, comforting sounds that made him feel at home in the cozy space, alongside the close-knit family. But it wasn't the same without Naomi at his side.

Gideon snuck a look over his shoulder. Naomi was wiping down the milking equipment with disinfectant. The sharp lemon scent reminded him of the Saturday before a visiting Sunday when he was a child and his mother would scrub the house until it shone. Back when his parents were still alive.

Naomi's hair was hidden beneath a blue work kerchief instead of a prayer *kapp* and she had a smudge of dirt on her cheek. She looked perfect. She was genuine and beautiful no matter what she was doing or how she was dressed. He turned back to the milking table and tried to force his attention back to his work.

He couldn't. Nothing was the same without Naomi nearby. At supper he tried to casually slide into the chair next to hers but she stepped back from her place right before she sat down. "I forgot the salt," she said and doubled back to the counter.

"It's right here." Leah picked up the saltshaker on the table, then set it down again.

"*Ach*, silly me." Naomi shrugged, then flashed a smile. When she came back to the table, she pulled out the chair where Miriam usually sat and plopped down fast. Miriam looked surprised for an instant, then pleased. Gideon watched with a slow, sinking feeling as Miriam took Naomi's usual spot—right beside him. Gideon tried not to sigh too loudly as she settled into place. This was going to be a very long dinner.

The home-cooked chicken casserole almost made up for the long, painful silence surrounding him throughout the meal. Almost, but not quite. He could not shake the feeling that Naomi was avoiding him on purpose. If he was honest with himself, it wasn't just a feeling, it was an observation. Worst of all, she was acting as if everything was fine. She and Benjamin chatted and laughed while she devoured everything on her plate. Meanwhile, Gideon was stuck in a bubble of silence between Miriam and Amanda. Amanda was too busy talking to David about an upcoming livestock auction to speak to Gideon. And Miriam only spoke to him in order to ask a few questions that left him unsettled.

"What are your plans after this?" she asked.

"Uh, I'm not sure." He set down his fork and reached for his glass of ice water. "Maybe stick around here for a while."

Miriam kept looking at him without responding. He didn't like it when people did that. It felt like they were trying to make him uncomfortable, or trying to get more information. And it worked every time. He felt too awkward during long silences like that, which made him too quick to blurt out more than he should say.

He didn't want Miriam to think that he expected to stay at Stoneybrook Farm so he added, "I mean, here in Lancaster County. Bluebird Hills is nice. It seems like a good place to settle down." His eyes shot over to Naomi, then back down to his plate. He had not meant to look up at her. But when he thought about feeling welcomed, she was what came to mind. He hoped Miriam had not caught his slipup. Especially now that Naomi was working so hard to avoid him.

Miriam nodded and Gideon wondered what she was thinking. He knew he shouldn't care—and he didn't, not really. What he cared about was that Miriam had sway over Naomi. She could convince her to be wary of him. Maybe that was already happening. Maybe Naomi had bought into Miriam's suspicions. More importantly, Gideon knew that families mattered. He didn't want to come between Naomi and hers. He knew how painful it was to lose family and he never wanted that to happen to Naomi, even if it meant that he had to step back from her. Even if he had to walk away.

The thought sent a ripple of unease through him. His two weeks were slipping by fast. With so little time, every moment counted and he did not want to lose even one minute with Naomi. Plus, how could he work out his feelings for her if they weren't spending time together? He could see himself falling for her, but he needed to get to know her better.

Sure, he liked the idea of love at first sight, but this was the real world. He needed to be responsible.

Gideon took a long, slow sip of water. As he set the glass back down, he risked another glance at Naomi. Her cheeks were flushed from the heat of the kitchen and she was still wearing her blue work kerchief. She ate a generous bite of chicken casserole, then waved her hand at Benjamin in a big, animated motion as she chewed, since she couldn't talk with her mouth full. She was so full of life. He could feel her energy and enthusiasm, even from a distance. He needed to figure out a way to spend more time with her.

No. He could not do that. If she was avoiding him—which she clearly was—then he would have to respect that. He would keep his distance because it was what she wanted. Even if his heart ached to be near to her.

The next morning, Gideon hurried to the goat shed. He did not linger in the kitchen to chat with Naomi over a cup of coffee before starting the chores. The sun was still below the horizon as he tramped across the farmyard with his mug in hand. The chilly, predawn air smelled of grass and fresh-cut hay. Hopefully, he could beat everyone to work that day and be out of the goat shed before Naomi arrived.

Gideon pushed open the wooden door and stepped into the warm, earthy space. Goats bleated and stumbled to their feet to stare at him with soft, black eyes. "Good morning," he said. "Ready for the milking?"

"Um, good morning," came a hesitant voice from behind a stack of hay bales. Naomi's voice. She stepped into view and sighed. "You're here early."

Gideon cringed. Now it looked like he was trying to grab time alone with her, when the opposite was true. "*Ya*. Thought I'd get a head start while all of you were drinking your *kaffi*."

Naomi smiled. The expression looked genuine, but she was probably just trying to be nice. She was kind like that. "I guess I had the same idea." She raised her mug, then took a sip. "Never too early to get to work."

"Never too early," Gideon repeated. The response felt lame. He took a big sip of coffee to cover the fact that he did not know what to say. Then he set the mug down on top of a crate. Here they were, alone together, which was exactly what he wanted until last night, when she began avoiding him. Now he would have to pretend that he preferred not to be here, with her, in order to respect her wishes. And save himself the rejection too, if he were honest with himself.

Gideon could not blame her. It was only natural for her to listen to her family and be wary of a stranger with a criminal record. He took off his straw hat and scratched his head as he thought through what to say. "I noticed that one of the fence posts looks a little shaky. Since you're already here to start on the milking, I can take a look at that. Wouldn't want one of the goats to get out today."

Gideon did not stick around long enough to gauge Naomi's reaction. He knew that if he did, his resolve might break down. He might even tell her how he really felt, which would be a disaster. So he pushed down his emotions, gave her a quick nod, and headed outside.

Chapter Seven

Naomi knew that Gideon was avoiding her. It was painfully obvious. He had practically run out of the goat shed when he realized that she was there. He must have gone there extra early to get away from her in the first place. The look on his face when she stepped out from behind the stack of hay bales said it all. Her breath had caught in her throat when she realized that they were alone together. She had been thrilled to see him.

But Gideon had not returned her smile. He had not seemed happy to see her. Instead, he had made up a ridiculous excuse about fixing the fence. John took care of that kind of work, since he had worked in construction for the *Englisch*, before coming back to the Amish. If there were any repairs to be done, John would have already been on it. And besides, they never did those kinds of jobs until the milking was done.

And so she had lost her opportunity to steal a private moment with Gideon before her sisters arrived. She had wanted to tell him that she needed to avoid him for a while, but only in front of her family. She had been pretty stealthy about it the day before—giving up her seat beside him to grab the salt had been a good idea—so he probably had not noticed yet.

Now, she had to face the fact that *he* was the one avoiding *her*. Had she imagined their connection up to now? Sure, he was the strong silent type—her favorite type in the Amish romance novels she read—so she was sure that she knew how to read him. But had she actually gotten it wrong?

She spent the milking rehashing all of their conversations. Had she always been the one to speak first? To smile first? Was he simply following her lead? Was he just being friendly? He seemed the type to be thoughtful like that.

The milking machine whirred in the background when a terrible thought entered her mind. Maybe he felt sorry for her. She gasped and straightened up. The nanny goat on the milking table looked up at her and bleated. Naomi gave her an absentminded pat on the head. Her mind was reeling. When she read an Amish romance novel, she always imagined herself as the heroine. But what if she were actually the sidekick? The quirky friend who was never the main character, only the comic relief?

Was that *her*?

"You *oll recht*?"

Naomi looked over to see Miriam staring at her. "*Ya*. Of course."

Miriam narrowed her eyes and studied Naomi for a moment before turning back to the goat on her own milking table.

"You look like you've seen a ghost," Amanda said as she unlatched a goat and patted her on the side. The nanny trotted down the ramp as Amanda reached for another one to take her place.

"What? *Nee*. I was just thinking."

"*Vell*, don't think too hard," Benjamin said. "We can't have that."

All of her siblings laughed.

"What are you thinking about?" Amanda asked. "How to find an Amish Prince Charming?"

Another round of laughter.

Naomi scowled at Amanda. "Of course not. I was thinking about Gideon and—"

"You're right, he's definitely *not* an Amish Prince Charming," Miriam muttered.

"I heard that!" Naomi said.

Miriam shrugged without taking her attention from the milking.

"I wasn't thinking about him in *that* way." Naomi hoped this wasn't a lie. She decided it was not because she was not thinking about marrying him, she was just thinking about how he wasn't sweet on her, which meant he could not, by definition, be her Amish Prince Charming. "I was thinking about how he's working alone this morning. I'm not sure he feels *willkumm*."

"We've taken him in," Miriam said. "Despite his being a stranger."

"We're required to take in strangers," Naomi said. "The scriptures are very clear on that. We're not going above and beyond. We're doing the basics of our faith."

Miriam frowned as she adjusted the milking equipment. The diesel-powered machine hummed quietly in the background. "Look, let's not make this more complicated than it has to be. You've done a *gut* job pulling back from him."

"Don't you care about how he feels?" Naomi asked.

"Of course I do. But I care about you too. About all of us. And I have to keep that in mind. We can be welcoming without being foolish."

"So you're saying I'm foolish?"

"*Nee*." Miriam leaned back from her milking table and sighed. "I'm saying you're…a dreamer."

"There's nothing wrong with that."

"There is when you dream the wrong dream and it leads

to trouble. I know you think that I was heartless to cut off my courtship, back when our parents died but—"

"I'm sorry, Miriam," Naomi interrupted it. "I didn't mean to say that."

"I know you didn't. But it's what you think, even if you didn't mean to say it out loud."

Naomi opened her mouth to argue, then closed it again. She did think that. So there was no way to deny it without lying.

"But *danki* for the apology. It's *oll recht*." Miriam turned her attention to Benjamin as he hunched over a milking table. "Why don't you see if Gideon needs help with whatever he's doing."

"He's checking on the fence," Benjamin said without looking up.

"Then find John and bring him with you," Miriam said, still looking at Benjamin. "You two can make him feel welcome, ain't so?"

"Sure can." Benjamin flipped off his milking machine, pushed back the crate he was sitting on, and stood up. "First thing I'll do is ask Gideon if he's sweet on Naomi."

"Don't you dare!" Naomi and Miriam said in unison.

Benjamin chuckled before strolling out the door.

When Naomi went outside to hang the laundry later that morning, she caught sight of Gideon beside the fence line, hammer in hand. John was studying one of the slats while Benjamin stared off into space. Ollie the guard dog loped over to Benjamin, who crouched down to scratch him behind the ears.

Naomi folded a white sheet over the line and clipped it in place with a clothespin. The wind whipped against the fabric, sending the scent of freshly washed linens billowing through the air. Naomi breathed in the clean detergent smell as she watched Gideon. He looked so handsome and mysterious as he stood there in silence, the wind ruffling his reddish-brown hair. The sun shone brightly against the hillside behind him and puffy white clouds soared across a brilliant blue sky. It would be a perfect day—if he were not avoiding her.

Naomi glanced around. No one else was near. She stared at Gideon as she hung a pillowcase without looking at it. She pulled a spare clothespin from between her lips and fastened it over the line, eyes still focused on the distance.

Gideon must have felt the eyes on him, because he turned his head to return her gaze. Their eyes locked. She started to smile, but he jerked his eyes away before she could. Then he turned away, so she could no longer see his expression. He was definitely sending a signal. And not a good one.

Another breeze whipped through the farmyard and the pillowcase on the line went flying into the air. She had not clipped it in. While she was busy staring at Gideon, she had missed the pillowcase and fastened the pin to the bare line. She watched it fly through the air, then drop to the ground as soon as the wind died down. Naomi sighed. Maybe Miriam was right. She dreamed too much. She couldn't even put clothes on the line without getting distracted.

Gideon glanced over his shoulder and saw the pillowcase lying on the ground, halfway between them. He looked around, dropped his hammer onto the grass, and jogged toward it. Naomi hitched up her skirt and hurried to meet him. Her heart was beating fast when she reached him, and not just from exertion.

"Need some help?" He scooped up the pillowcase and handed it to her.

"*Ach, nee*. I'm fine."

Gideon nodded. They stared at one another for a moment.

He was probably thinking about how silly she was. He had caught her watching him while he stood beside the fence, and now he was having to chase down flying pillowcases for her. She was a mess and everyone could see that.

"We're going over the fence line today. Just checking to make sure it's secure."

She was glad he had broken the silence first. "It's a *gut* day to do that. *Vell*, a little too windy, maybe." Naomi cringed inside. They had been reduced to talking about the weather. They were getting farther and farther away from their earlier connection.

"*Ya*." Gideon winked at her. "Better watch out. Pillowcases are flying around."

Naomi froze for an instant. Had he just made a joke? She grinned. Her heart was beating even faster than before. What should she say in return?

"*Vell*, best get back to work," Gideon said. She watched him march back to the fence and pick up his hammer before she turned away. How had she let him slip away without saying something, *anything*?

Being near Gideon was just too confusing.

Gideon was kicking himself. He must seem like a fool. What was Naomi thinking about him now? Nothing good, that was certain sure. In the heat of the moment, he had made a bad joke, then winked at her. Winked! What kind of man winked at a woman? Nobody did that in real life, not seriously.

And yet, he had. He was awful at this. He simply could not talk to a woman he was sweet on. Especially if she were avoiding him. He had gathered all his courage and sent out an enormous hint to test the water and try to bridge the gap. But the wink, and the joke, had fallen flat. She had just stared at him as if he had done something utterly ridiculous. Sure, she had managed a smile, but that was obviously out of discomfort. Or perhaps she didn't want to hurt his feelings. Either way, the message had been clear. He was an oaf.

Gideon decided the only course of action was to double down on avoiding Naomi. He never should have run to help her. But what else could he have done? He wanted to make her life easier. He wanted to show that he cared. He wanted her to feel special.

He needed to push those desires aside. Hadn't he learned his lesson over the years? People did not stay in his life. Relationships could not be trusted. They were not permanent. He was getting too soft, and it would only lead to heartbreak. He needed to toughen up and put the walls back up. He had always been good at that.

The problem was that, inexplicably, Naomi had chipped away at that wall's foundation. Now, it wasn't so easy to put it up again. He could barely keep from staring at her when he ran into her that evening. She was headed from the goat shed to the production building, hauling a metal bucket full of milk in each hand. He tried to force his eyes to stay on the chicken coop in the distance. But he was drawn to her like a magnet, unable to resist.

His gaze slid to her against his will. Her eyes were bright, her cheeks ruddy from heat and exertion. She looked so cheerful and full of life, even while working. Their eyes met and she started to smile, then looked away quickly. He could see her straining to carry the heavy buckets and, even though he wanted to give her space, he could not resist offering to help. It would be wrong to stand by while she struggled.

Naomi skipped a step to avoid a red hen, then stumbled to regain her balance. Milk sloshed over the top of the buckets. Gideon jumped into action and sprinted to her. "Let me help you."

"*Ach*, it's fine. I do this all the time."

Gideon nodded. He didn't want to be patronizing. She was a hard worker, and clearly able to do whatever needed to be done. "I know you can do it yourself, but I'd rather do it while I'm here. It doesn't seem right for me to stand here and watch you carry something, when I'm right here to help."

Naomi stared up at him.

His heart stopped for a moment. The farmyard went silent, the barking dog and clucking chickens fading into the distance. Because Naomi was gazing into his eyes like he was some kind of hero. Her mouth was parted slightly, her eyes wide, and brighter than before. Or maybe she was just surprised. After all, she had been trying to keep her distance and he should have gotten the hint by now.

"You really mean that?"

"Of course. Here." He reached for the buckets. She slipped them into his hands without breaking eye contact. He smiled and so did she. They both stood there for few beats. He didn't want to tear himself away. No one had ever looked at him like that before.

"*Danki*," she said after a moment.

Gideon remembered to feel self-conscious. He should not jump to conclusions. One look was not enough to go on, no matter how riveting it had been. "So, this goes in there?" He nodded behind him, toward the big sheet metal building in the backyard.

"*Recht. Ya.*" Naomi looked like she had just been startled awake. "In the production building." The ruddiness on her cheeks deepened into a blush.

"Okay," Gideon said. "No problem."

They walked in silence, side by side. Ollie trotted over, circled them, then sniffed one of the buckets.

"*Gut bu*," Naomi murmured and scratched behind his ears. He trotted alongside them for a moment, then his ears pricked and he darted away, toward something they could not see or hear.

Gideon was painfully aware of Naomi's closeness as they crossed the muddy farmyard and passed behind the house. He could hear her breath beside his ear and the soft thud of her footsteps against the damp earth. He kept trying to think of something clever and charming to say, but they reached the big double doors of the production building before anything came to mind.

"I can take it from here," Naomi said. She pulled open one of the doors and cool air rushed out to meet them, along with the quiet hum of diesel-powered machinery.

"It's no trouble for me to take it all the way in."

Naomi glanced inside, then back at him, as she braced the door open with her hip. He could hear voices inside, followed by the clang of metal against metal. "That's *oll recht*," Naomi said. "I've got it."

Gideon hesitated, then handed over the buckets. He could see her slump forward from the weight and wished she would let him finish the job. But it was clear that she didn't want him to come inside. Maybe she didn't want her sisters to see them together. That would make sense. She would not want them to think that she was sweet on him. He'd seen that happen before, when people assumed that a woman was sweet on a man, when she was just trying to be kind. Naomi was that sort of woman, kind to strangers.

The door shut and the cool interior of the production building disappeared, along with Naomi. He was left staring at the sheet metal wall, wondering if there could be another option. Was it possible that she *was* sweet on him? Was she trying to hide her feelings from her siblings?

It was a nice thought. But not a realistic one. Better to keep those daydreams away and stick to reality. He was a temporary hired hand and that was all he would ever be to Naomi or the rest of her family.

Chapter Eight

Naomi was so confused. Gideon had obviously been avoiding her. But then, he swooped in and carried the milk buckets for her. That was the second time that day he had come to her aid. What was happening?

He was a good man, that was what. He was kind and thoughtful. He wasn't going to stand by and watch her struggle. That was just the way he was. It didn't mean that he was sweet on her.

And yet, she couldn't help but feel a spark of hope. She obsessed over it as she drove the buggy to the Feed & Seed to restock supplies. Stalks of wheat rippled in the breeze as golden rays of sun winked across the brown-and-yellow fields. She passed the one-room Amish schoolhouse and saw the children playing volleyball in the yard. The girls' emerald, ruby, and lilac dresses looked like spring wildflowers against the bright green grass. She could hear their laughter, carried on the wind.

Naomi could envision her own child going to that school one day. Would it be a daughter, or a little boy—

Naomi cut off the thought. This was not the time to be daydreaming about future children with a man who might not even be interested.

But then again, he might be.

Her gut and her brain tugged against one another as she turned onto Bluebird Hill's main street. Clyde plodded along, his hooves clattering against the pavement, as they passed the coffee shop and bookstore. Downtown had a quaint, old-fashioned look, with mom-and-pop shops in a row. An *Englisch* couple wearing jeans and T-shirts stopped to wave. Naomi smiled and waved back. Some Amish folk didn't like having so many tourists around, but she didn't mind. She liked that they appreciated her way of life.

Clyde trotted past Beiler's Quilt and Fabric Shop. The window in the yellow-and-white storefront was filled with displays of plain, solid fabrics. She reached a stop sign and tugged on the reins. "Whoa."

An Amish woman on a push scooter with a plastic grocery bag in one hand crossed the street in front of them. Naomi flicked the reins and Clyde went through the intersection, then turned into a parking space for buggies in front of a square brick building painted white. A faded wooden sign with the words FEED & SEED stretched across the front.

The Feed & Seed had been there since her grandparents' time and stepping inside was like going back to the days before the *Englisch* hustle and bustle took over the area. The family-run shop had electricity and a fancy cash register, of course. But it still had a barrel of old-fashioned penny candy beside the dinted wooden counter, floors that creaked, and stacks of burlap sacks that filled the air with a familiar, earthy scent.

"Hey there," Billy Tyler, the shopkeeper, said from behind the counter as the bell rang over Naomi's head. "How's the family?" He had on the same frayed baseball cap he always wore.

"Everyone's good."

"Those little ones are growing fast." He closed the cash

register drawer and leaned against the counter. "I couldn't believe how big Caleb was when Benjamin and Emma brought him in last week."

Naomi smiled. "For certain sure."

There was a loud tapping against the wooden floorboards from somewhere across the store. Naomi had a pretty good idea who that must be.

"So, what do you need today?" Billy asked.

There was another loud tap and Viola Esch appeared around the corner of the tall wooden shelves. "I think I'm being summoned."

Billy chuckled. "Well, I won't get in your way, Viola." He nodded to Naomi. "Let me know if you need anything."

"Danki."

Viola waved Naomi over with her cane. She looked frail and stooped, but purpose flashed in her eyes. Naomi knew what this would be about. In fact, the only surprise was that Viola had not showed up on her doorstep yet. She always found a way to share her opinion.

"What a nice surprise running into you here," Naomi said as she padded across the shop floor.

"Not really a surprise," Viola said. "I knew there would be a *gut* chance of finding a Stoltzfus here. Why do you think I came in to get seeds for my garden today? One of you always shows up the afternoon that Billy restocks. Two errands taken care of in one place."

"Right." Naomi straightened her starched white apron. She didn't want Viola to point out any winkles. "But you didn't know which one of us might show up."

Viola shrugged. "Any of you would do. But you're the one I was hoping to see the most."

"Oh."

Viola waved her cane at Naomi. "Don't play coy with me. You know I'm going to ask you about Gideon."

"Ya."

"So, tell me what's going on."

"Um. Nothing?"

Viola cackled. "No lying."

Naomi sighed. "He's a *gut* worker. No complaints."

Viola waved a bony hand. "I know that. I'm asking how it's going between you and him."

Naomi sighed again.

"You were mighty quick to defend him at the work frolic."

"It was the right thing to do. You defended him too."

"That's irrelevant. We're talking about how *you're* sweet on him."

Naomi flinched. "Is that what we're talking about?"

"Of course. I wasn't born yesterday, dear. Now, tell me how it's going between you two. Has he asked to court you yet?"

"*Nee*. It's not like that."

Viola raised her eyebrows.

"Really, it's not."

"Sounds like I'll have to pay a visit and talk to Miriam. She's giving you a hard time about it, I imagine."

"There's no need for that."

"There obviously is. But you need to be understanding about it. Things haven't been easy for her."

Naomi shifted her weight from one foot to the other. "I know."

"Just leave it to me."

Naomi could feel control slipping away from her. "It's not that. You don't understand."

Viola narrowed her eyes as she studied Naomi's expression. "Then what is it?"

"I'm not sure how Gideon feels about me." Naomi squeezed her eyes shut. Had she really just said that out loud—and to Viola, of all people? She had. The words had just slid out, before she could stop herself. Maybe she wanted someone to know. It had been eating her up to hold it all inside.

"*Vell*, have you asked him?"

Naomi stiffened. "*Nee*. Of course not."

"Pffft. *Youngies* today. How can you know how he feels if you don't ask him?"

"Because that would be too forward."

"That sounds like Miriam talking."

"*Vell…*"

"That's what I thought." Viola took a deep breath and let it out slowly. "Miriam's a *gut* woman, but she's not one to give advice when it comes to love. She doesn't know how to follow her own heart."

"Oh." No one had ever put it quite like that before.

"You don't agree?" Viola frowned as she stared at Naomi.

"Uh, *nee*." Naomi frowned. "I mean, yes, I do agree. But it's not something that I would say out loud."

"You don't have to. I said it for you."

Naomi blinked a few times. She did not know how to respond to that.

"Sometimes things have to be said."

"And you've never had trouble being the one to say it."

Viola smiled. "Someone has to."

Naomi wasn't sure that was always true. She didn't mind sweeping things under the rug sometimes, if it kept the peace.

Viola thumped the floor with her cane. "You can't hide from the truth forever."

"I'm not hiding."

"Just talk to him. He's a nice *bu*, you're a nice *maedel*. It doesn't have to be complicated."

"It's complicated if he doesn't have feelings for me."

Viola waved her hand. "It's obvious he's sweet on you."

Naomi straightened up. "What makes you say that?"

Viola rolled her eyes. "I'm old enough to know it when I see it. And Miriam probably sees it too, which is why she's giving you a hard time about it."

"But he's been avoiding me."

"That just proves my point. He's avoiding you because he's sweet on you."

"We're not children, Viola."

"That doesn't mean you can't act like one. Do I really have to spell it out? After all that *bu* has been through, he's probably too afraid to tell you how he really feels—and I'm sure Miriam isn't making it any easier for him."

Naomi's brow crinkled. "So, you really think he likes me?"

"Only one way to find out, ain't so?"

Naomi knew that Viola was right. And she also knew that she better take the advice right away, before she lost her courage—no matter how loud the warning bells sounded inside her head.

Gideon was crossing from the production building to the goat shed when he noticed the sunset. He stopped in the farmyard, an empty milk jug in his hand, and stared down the long, sloping hillside into the Yoders' land. The sun cast a soft orange glow over the lake at the bottom of the valley. A lone duck floated on the surface, sending ripples across the shimmering water. A sunflower field lay in front of the pond and the flowers swayed in the breeze like lazy dancers with bright yellow hats. Above it all, an azure sky was fading to pink as the day settled slowly into night. This was a view that he had always dreamed of seeing from his own land. What must it be like for the Stoltzfus family, waking up each day, knowing the land beneath their feet and the sky above their heads was theirs? Knowing they could look out every evening and see the simple beauty of God's creation in a sunset over a friendly neighbor's fields?

The sound of wheels crunching against gravel pulled Gideon out of the moment. He turned to see the buggy winding up the long driveway. Clyde trudged closer in a slow, steady rhythm as his hooves beat a familiar song against the earth. This was how Gideon had grown up—in a home where love and security were as expected as the steady thud of a horse's hoofbeats. Now, his heart ached to return—or to stay here, where he had recaptured the feeling.

Gideon knew who was driving the buggy before he could make out her face. He had noticed when Naomi left, though he had tried to act as if he were not paying attention. He hesitated. Should he go help her unload, even though he was supposed to be giving her space? He had overheard that she was going to the Feed & Seed to restock. His hesitation only lasted an instant. He could give her space after he hauled those heavy feed bags. There was no reason for her to do it herself.

Gideon set the empty milk jug onto the ground and jogged toward the buggy as it approached. A slender arm appeared from the window and waved. Gideon grinned and waved back. He had done the right thing. Or at least, Naomi was going to be friendly, even if she was annoyed with him.

The buggy pulled into the farmyard in a cloud of dust. "I'll give you a hand," Gideon said as he approached.

"*Danki*." Naomi pushed open the buggy door and dropped to the ground. Her face was red and Gideon wondered if she was flushed from heat or if something was wrong. She looked down and smoothed down her apron.

"Everything *oll recht*?"

Naomi's head jerked back up. "*Ya.* Of course. Why wouldn't it be?"

Gideon shrugged. "Uh, no reason." He frowned and cleared his throat. "I'll see to those feed bags."

Naomi nodded, but she did not turn away. Instead, her attention stayed on his face.

Gideon didn't pull his gaze away either. She looked so beautiful, silhouetted against the setting sun, the skirt of her dress rippling in the breeze.

She squeezed her eyes shut. "I may as well say it now."

"Say what?"

Her eyes opened, but her forehead remained crinkled, her lips tight. She scratched her arm, looked away, then met his eyes again. "Why have you been avoiding me? Or I guess I should ask, *have* you been avoiding me?"

"Is that what's bothering you?"

"How did you know something was bothering me?"

"Because you've got that little crinkle in your forehead. And your cheeks are flushed. And you can't stand still and look at me."

"Oh." The crease in Naomi's forehead deepened. "You've noticed all those things about me?"

Now it was Gideon's turn to look away. "*Ach*, I don't know. It just seemed obvious."

"It's not obvious to other people. No one else has ever said they noticed all those things before."

"They probably just didn't see any point in mentioning it. I'm sure people notice everything about you."

Naomi's cheeks flushed a darker shade of red and her eyes brightened. "Because you do?"

"Uh, *vell…*" Gideon took off his straw hat, ran his fingers through his hair, and pushed it back down again. This was the time to either make an excuse or to throw out a hint. Was he brave enough to tell Naomi that he noticed everything about her because he could not get enough of her? That being near her was like taking a good, long drink on a sweltering day?

No, of course he would not say all of that. She would laugh in his face. He had to stop being such a silly romantic. She would not want to hear it. Especially when he had nothing to offer her except for sweet words. Words could not put food on the table. Words could not convince a church district—or an overprotective family—that he was worthy.

She was still staring up at him with that adorable crinkle in her forehead. "Do you?"

"I've noticed you—I mean, things about you." He did not want to say too much, but he did not want to leave her hanging either. His throat was tight and his mouth felt dry. He had never been this forward before. He had never come close to courting a woman before.

Not that they were close to courting. He was getting way ahead of himself. "I mean, you're noticeable." Gideon cringed. He had not meant to say that. It had come out all wrong. As always, the more he said, the deeper hole he dug. He had to get out of this, fast. "You're loud. I mean, not loud. Or not loud in a bad way. You're enthusiastic. You say what you're thinking."

"I'm loud?" Naomi shrunk a little.

"*Nee*, that's not what I meant." He took off his straw hat again and slapped it against his thigh. "This isn't easy."

"What isn't easy?"

"To tell you that I like spending time with you. That I like…you."

Naomi gasped. "You do?"

Gideon swallowed hard. "*Ya.* I do." He felt completely exposed, as if he were in a room full of people and they were all staring at him. Except it was only Naomi. But that didn't feel any different, because she was the only person whose opinion mattered.

The crinkle between Naomi's eyes disappeared and her face brightened. "Really and truly?"

Gideon smiled. She did not seem embarrassed or irritated. She did not seem like she was trying to avoid the subject. Instead, she was glowing. Was this what she had been longing to hear? "Really and truly." He said the words in a deep, even voice, then stared at her, waiting for her response.

She clasped her hands together and brought them against her chest. "Oh! I like you too!"

"Oh." Gideon knew he should say more, but he was too shocked by her declaration. She liked him? Shouldn't she be scared away by his past? Shouldn't she look down on him? Or play hard to get?

No, Naomi wasn't like that. She was authentic and true. She saw him for who he was and that was enough for her. And he saw her for the way she was and it was enough for him. Could this be real? Could this be happening? Surely it was a dream that he would wake up from. It was too unexpected, too good.

Naomi laughed. "We sound like schoolchildren."

Gideon smiled. "Like when they write notes asking, if you like me check the 'yes' box?"

Naomi laughed again. "*Ya*, like that."

Gideon laughed too. It felt good to let out some of his nervous energy. He desperately wanted to sweep her up into his arms, hold her close, and whisper into her ear that he had never felt this way about anyone else. He wanted to feel her heartbeat against his and smell the lavender scent that clung to her hair. But he stayed still. It might be too much. They only admitted to liking one another. He knew that his feelings went deeper than that, but he didn't want to say too much too soon. They were still practically strangers. More importantly, they were standing in the middle of the farmyard. Anyone could be watching. He could only imagine what would happen if her siblings caught him hugging her right there, in plain sight. He would probably be out on the street again before morning.

Naomi took a step closer. He wondered if she wanted him to take her in his arms. There was a warmth in her eyes that said she did. "What happens now?" she asked, her gaze locked on him.

He swallowed hard. "I don't know." He glanced around the farmyard, then back to her. "We spend as much time as we can together, while we can. We see where it goes."

Naomi smiled. "I thought you were avoiding me."

"I thought *you* were avoiding *me*."

They both laughed. It felt good to be in sync. It felt good to understand one another.

"I was trying to respect you and give you space," Gideon said.

"I was trying to keep Miriam from thinking that we liked each other."

Gideon nodded. "I wondered about that."

"You thought I didn't want to spend time with you?"

Gideon raised his hands, palms up. "I wasn't sure."

Naomi shook her head. "That wasn't it at all."

"I see that now." Her brown eyes were so rich and deep that he felt like he might fall into them.

They stared at one another without speaking. Gideon could hear his heartbeat pounding in his ears and was certain that he could sense hers.

"Naomi!" Miriam's voice called out across the farmyard.

They jerked apart and swung their heads toward the goat shed.

"You got the feed?" Miriam asked from the doorway of the building, an empty burlap sack in her hand.

"*Ya*!" Naomi called back.

"I'll get it," Gideon said, loudly enough for his voice to carry, then nodded at Naomi before heading to the back of the buggy.

His hands were soon busy with work, but his mind could only focus on one thing. *What happens now?*

Chapter Nine

Naomi was overflowing with joy. She wanted to sing and shout. She wanted tell everyone that the mysterious man who had arrived on their doorstep *was* her Amish Prince Charming. She had known that this was it. Sure, her sisters would remind her of other times when she had gotten swept away by hope and emotion, but this time was different. She just knew it. It was different because Gideon was different. He had no ulterior motives. He did not brag or act like a know-it-all in order to impress her. He was quiet and thoughtful, reserved and kind. He was the man whom she had been waiting for while dreaming about her wedding day.

Of course, she had not told Gideon all of that. Even she was not forward enough to announce to him that she had already visualized their wedding. She knew exactly which dress she would wear—the new pink one—and that she would serve apple crumble with peppermint swirl ice cream on top, because that was her favorite dessert. She would have to ask him what flavor of ice cream he liked best.

It was hard to hide her excitement from her family. She tried to play down her mood, but it was impossible. The birds sounded sweeter, the sun looked brighter, and she felt as if she were floating two feet above the ground as she walked. When she was sure no one was looking, Naomi twirled in a circle with her arms spread wide to feel the romantic swoosh of her dress against her legs and release her excitement. Benjamin caught her when he walked into the goat shed without warning, but Naomi rushed past him before he could question her.

"What are you doing?" Benjamin asked. She was already at the doorway, cheeks flushed from the day's excitement. Had it been less than an hour since she and Gideon had admitted that they liked each other?

"*Ach*, nothing," Naomi said without turning back.

"Something's different about you," Benjamin said.

"Mmm, *vell*, gotta go."

"Why don't you go walk my *boppli* until he falls asleep. You've got all that extra energy and I'm worn out."

"I'd be happy to." She could twirl Caleb around and sing and no one would suspect a thing.

Benjamin raised his eyebrows. "So you don't have anything else to do."

"What do you mean?"

"You just said you had to go."

"Ya."

Benjamin laughed and shook his head. "Something's going on with you."

Naomi just shrugged and smiled before slipping away. She could hear Caleb crying inside the farmhouse before she reached the door. The noise drifted through the open kitchen window and into the night. Naomi hummed as she followed the cries and found Emma balancing Caleb on her hip while rummaging through the refrigerator. Her face lit up when Naomi offered to give her a break. "I've been trying to put him down for a while and nothing is working. He's full of energy tonight. I gave up and came downstairs to get myself a glass of milk."

Caleb's little face was red and his hands were curled into fists.

"He's so adorable when he cries," Naomi said.

Emma looked down at her son. Her smile broadened. "He sure is." She kissed him on the nose before passing him over to Naomi.

She tucked him close and wandered toward the front door, pressing her cheek against his and humming softly in his ear. She inhaled the sweet scent of baby as she opened the screen door with her free hand, let it slam behind her, and trotted down the front porch steps.

The night sky spread over the hills and pasturelands in a black velvet blanket with pinpricks of light. The darkness filled the farmyard and allowed the stars to shine bright and true. Naomi thought about how sailors used to use the stars to navigate across vast oceans, with no land in sight. "Be my north star, *Gott*," she whispered. "Guide my future with Gideon." Her eyes cut from the sky to the *dawdi haus*. The windows flickered yellow with lantern light, so she knew that he was inside. She could imagine walking up the stairs one day, after they were married, their own baby in her arms. It felt right. Naomi took a deep breath and let it out slowly as she smiled into the quiet darkness. Deep inside, she knew that if that were true, and this really was right, *Gott* would see it through. And she was almost positive that it was right.

Except for that little nagging warning inside, reminding her that she had chosen poorly before. That she had no judgment when it came to men. That she was too naive and trusting and had suffered the consequences before. But Gideon was not like that.

Because he couldn't be.

She had no better reason that that.

A breeze rippled through a neighboring wheat field and

swept through the farmyard, rustling the leaves of the oak tree beside the house. She shivered and hoped that the chill was only from the wind. Caleb shifted in her arms. He had stopped crying and was gazing up at the dome of stars above them. Ollie barked in a distant pasture and the goats bleated. Other than that, the night was still and silent, the chickens tucked away in their coop, the two border collies sleeping beneath the front porch.

Naomi kissed the top of Caleb's head. "*Vell*, there's only one way to find out if Gideon is who I think he is. I've got to spend more time with him." Caleb gurgled in response. Naomi smiled as she marched to the *dawdi haus*, pounded up the steps, and knocked.

When the door swung open, Gideon's grin looked so honest, so genuine. His brown hair was disheveled and he wasn't wearing his straw hat. She could imagine coming home to him like this, casual and comfortable around one another.

"Hi," he said.

Neither one spoke for a moment after that. Naomi knew she should say something, but now she felt sheepish.

"Is, uh, everything *oll recht*?"

"*Ya*. Everything's *gut*. Just trying to help Caleb settle down." She patted the baby's back and he snuggled closer.

Gideon nodded. He looked like he wanted to say something, but didn't.

Naomi felt her cheeks flush with heat. "So, I was walking by and just thought, *vell*, maybe you want to *kumme* walk with us? It's a beautiful night and—"

"Just let me get my hat," Gideon cut in.

Naomi felt her body relax. She had not realized how tense she was until he said yes. And he must have known that she was nervous, because he didn't let her fumble through her invitation. He jumped in and said he wanted to step out with her.

Wait. Did this mean they were literally stepping out now? Were they courting?

No, surely not. This wasn't the way that worked. He would need to ask her outright. They would go out in the courting buggy together for a Sunday drive after a church service. Of course, they had already been out in the courting buggy together. Alone. But that had not meant anything. And, earlier this evening, he had admitted that he liked her. Should she ask him outright if they were courting? No, Miriam would have a fit. Women did not ask men to court. If Naomi had her way, she would change that rule. She knew exactly what she wanted, so why shouldn't she have some say in it?

Because it would be scandalous, that's why. And Miriam would never let her forget about it. Neither would the rest of the church district when they found out about it—and they *would* find out about it. Somehow, they always found out about everything.

Naomi startled when Gideon reappeared at the door with his straw hat in his hand. She had been so deep in thought, she had almost forgotten where she was. Too much daydreaming, her family always told her. But daydreaming was nice, so why not indulge in it? And how could she keep her head out of the clouds when Gideon's earlier declaration was still making her feel like she was floating? There was so much to consider, so much to obsess over. And she loved every minute of it. There was nothing so wonderful as that deep surge of joy that only love could bring.

Gideon smiled, popped his hat onto his head, stepped through the doorway, and closed the door behind him in a quiet thump. "You look happy," he said.

"I am happy."

Gideon watched her for a moment, but said nothing. She sensed that he wanted to say or ask something, and wondered what it was. Caleb whimpered and pushed against her chest. "We better get walking," Naomi said. "He likes the movement."

"Still teething?" Gideon asked as he followed her down the two porch steps.

"*Ya*. Poor thing."

"You want me to take a turn?"

"If you want to."

"*Ya*, I do."

Their hands touched as she passed Caleb to him. He paused for an instant and looked directly into her eyes as his warm skin rested against hers. Naomi's breath caught in her chest. Then Gideon bundled Caleb into his arms and the moment was gone. But not forgotten. Naomi would store that moment of connection in her heart to remember for a very long time.

Gideon looked upward. "It's beautiful tonight."

"Ya."

Gideon's eyes flicked to hers, then back up to the sky. "I've seen the stars above so many different farms. One day, I want to see them above my own farm."

"Is that your dream? To have your own farm?"

"*Ya*." He sighed and rubbed Caleb's back. "We never had one when I was growing up. I guess I told you that already. But we had a little house and a small plot of land. There was an oak tree, like that one." He nodded toward the dark silhouette rising above the farmhouse. "And a lake nearby."

"Like the one down there?" Naomi looked down the long, sloping hillside, to the bottom of the Yoder land, but saw nothing except the soft, sweep of darkness. Everything was sleeping, it seemed. She felt like they were the only people awake in the world.

"*Ya*. But without the sunflower field. The one I grew up beside had a feed corn field nearby. And a creek with a little red footbridge." He breathed in deeply and let it out. It was perfect. Or it seemed like it. "I was a child, and the world felt different back then."

Naomi nodded as she stared into the darkness. "I know what you mean. When I was a child, no one minded that I kept my head in the clouds. But now they say I need to grow up and keep two feet on the ground." She exhaled. "Miriam has lots of sayings like that."

Gideon smiled. His face looked silver in the moonlight. "I don't think you should change anything about you."

"You really mean that?"

He looked down and adjusted Caleb's blanket. "*Ya*. Hope you don't mind I said it."

"*Nee*, I don't mind at all."

Wind whistled up the hillside and rippled through the skirt of Naomi's dress. A goat bleated in a distant field. Naomi could not believe that she was standing beneath the stars with Gideon. Just the two of them. Well, three, if you counted Caleb. Naomi smiled to herself. No one could say they didn't have a chaperone. "Tell me about the farm you hope to have one day." This was her chance to get to know him better, without interruptions from nosy siblings.

Gideon smiled. His eyes took on a faraway look. "*Vell*, it's a lot like Stoneybrook Farm. I always wanted a lake nearby, just like when I was growing up. And I wanted it to have a good view, like this place does. It's nice being able to see down the hill from here. The sunset was beautiful today.

"You noticed that?"

"*Ya*. Of course I did. It lit up the sky and the lake..." Gideon gave a sheepish shrug.

"I've never heard a man talk about sunsets like that."

He kicked at the dirt with the toe of his black work boot.

"I like that about you," Naomi said.

Gideon's attention jerked up from the ground. "You do?"

"For certain sure. Everyone should appreciate things like that, don't you think?"

"*Ya*. I do." Gideon chuckled, then shook his head.

"What?"

"I don't think I've ever met anyone like you, Naomi."

"Oh. *Vell*, I don't think I've ever met anyone like you either." The men who had tried to court her before had never talked about sunsets or shared dreams or childhood memories. She had been waiting her entire life to find someone who saw the same beauty in the world that she did, and was not afraid to share it with others. "Tell me more about your dreams."

"I always wanted a big, rambling farmhouse full of family."

"Like this one?" Naomi nodded toward her home with its creaky floorboards, whitewashed walls, and tin roof.

"*Ya*. Just like this one. The double porch is a nice added touch. I hadn't thought of that."

"What about goats? You like them?"

Gideon laughed. "Never gave much thought to that either. But I've liked working with them."

"So you envisioned growing crops instead of raising animals?"

Gideon thought for a moment. "I guess I never figured it mattered much, one way or the other. I've been dreaming about the land, the house..." He hesitated, then added, "... the family."

Naomi's heart dropped to her toes, then shot back up again. Was he hinting about her being his family one day? About her siblings and in-laws being his in-laws one day? "Maybe you can stay a while."

"*Ach*, I don't know about that. Katie's parents will be back soon, ain't so? Then I'll have to move out of the *dawdi haus*."

"I could talk to the rest of the family. There's room in the farmhouse."

Gideon shifted Caleb from one shoulder to the other. "I'm not sure that will go so well."

"There's only one way to find out."

"Maybe leave well enough alone for now."

"You're afraid Miriam will be against it."

"Maybe it's best not to give her a chance to say no just yet. Give it some time. I'm still a stranger."

Naomi turned to face him. Part of his face was hidden in shadow, but she could make out his eyes, as warm and clear as ever. "You're not a stranger to me. Not anymore."

In fact, Naomi wasn't sure that he ever had been. She had always wanted to believe that love at first sight was real, no matter how much everyone else told her that it was foolish. Gideon was proving to her that all her romantic dreams were possible. Now, all she had to do was convince her family that their love was real—and worth fighting for.

Naomi could barely contain herself. It was all she could do to stay quiet until she found a moment alone with her sisters the next day. She didn't want to bring it up in front of Gideon, of course. That would be too awkward for him. Especially if they reacted poorly. But they had to react well. They just had to.

She followed Miriam and Amanda to the production building after the morning milking and slipped inside the big double doors. The familiar whirr of machinery filled the open space. On the other side of the shiny metal vats, refrigerator doors thumped open and closed. “Miriam?”

“*Ya*?” The voice carried across the building.

“Um, I was just looking for you.”

“*Vell*, I guess it wasn’t hard to find me since we always bring the milk here.”

Naomi laughed, but didn’t feel it inside. Her stomach was churning. But this shouldn’t be a big deal. Why should she be nervous to talk to her own sister? Especially when what she had to say was perfectly reasonable.

“Bring me the clipboard from the desk on your way over here,” Miriam said.

Naomi watched the distorted reflection of her body in the surface of the curved metal vat as she crossed the room. She looked big, then small; skinny, then fat. She wondered if everyone saw her as something different from what she really was. She knew that, inside, she was smart and discerning, even if everyone else saw her as foolish and naive.

“Where’s Leah and Amanda?” Naomi asked as she picked up the clipboard from the desk built into one of the long metal counters.

“I’m here,” Leah called out, followed by the thud of a door and the rattle of a metal bottle.

“So am I,” Amanda shouted.

“*Ach, gut*.” Naomi tried to look nonchalant as she turned the corner of the pasteurization equipment and saw her sisters standing in front of the row of refrigerators. The entire building ran on a generator and she could hear it humming softly outside, through the corrugated sheet metal walls. Leah picked a glass bottle of milk from a cart, opened one of the refrigerator doors, and set it on the shelf alongside a row of identical bottles. A whoosh of cold air rushed toward Naomi and she rubbed her bare arms.

"Naomi, I thought you were going to get started on the sourdough," Miriam said.

"I can't do it," Amanda said. "David and I are rotating the goats to a different pasture before lunch."

"No one is expecting you to do the baking, Amanda." Naomi laughed. "We all know you'd rather be outside, with the goats."

Amanda smiled. "Just making sure."

"Naomi's going to take care of the baking, right, Naomi?" Miriam asked.

"*Ya*, of course. I just wanted to talk to you all first."

Miriam reached for the clipboard in Naomi's hand. "Can it wait until lunch? We'll have more time then." She scanned the top page, then flipped up the paper to expose the second sheet. "I've got an order to get out this morning."

"Um, *nee*, it's better if Gideon's not here."

Miriam's eyes shot up to Naomi. "I'm listening."

Naomi smiled. She had Miriam's attention now. Of course, that meant that she had to plead her case, which might not go very well. Naomi cleared her throat. "*Vell*, I've been talking to Gideon."

Miriam sighed. "*Ya*. We know that."

"*Nee*, I mean we've been talking about him being here. He's really happy here."

Miriam's jaw flexed. "Because he thinks he has a chance with you?"

"Can you please set that aside for a minute? This is not about that."

"I wouldn't be so sure."

"Miriam, come on. Just listen to me." Miriam could be

so exasperating. And, the worst thing was, Miriam was almost always right.

But not this time. She just couldn't be.

Miriam sighed and dropped the clipboard onto the metal cart, where it landed with a clang. "Okay. I'm listening."

Naomi nodded. "*Gut*." She cleared her throat again. "Gideon is a hard worker. You can't argue that."

Leah nodded. "That's true."

"He's been a *gut* help," Amanda said. "He's a natural with the goats, that's for certain sure."

"And the babies," Naomi added.

Leah laughed. "And the babies. He's been great with Abby."

"So, I think we should let him stay longer." Naomi held her breath and waited for Miriam's reaction.

Miriam nodded slowly. "He has been a *gut* help."

"And we do need extra help since we combined David's herd with ours," Amanda said.

Leah pushed the cart aside and leaned her hip against the glass door of the industrial refrigerator. "Anyone who can get Caleb to settle down has got to be a good guy, ain't so?"

They all laughed.

"I mean, babies can sense those kinds of things, right?" Leah added.

"*Ach*, I don't know about that," Miriam said.

"Animals can definitely sense that," Naomi said. "Even Belinda likes him."

Leah raised her eyebrows. "That's hard to argue with, Miriam."

Miriam smiled, but it did not reach her eyes. "I appreciate the thought, but we're not going to make any decisions based on what a goose thinks."

"Okay, but what about based on what *I* think?" Naomi asked. "Can't you trust me?"

Miriam pinched the bridge of her nose. "*Ach*, Naomi, I want to. But you've got to prove that you can see these things."

"I don't need to prove anything to you." The indignation burned inside her chest. "I'm an adult, same as you. I'm perfectly capable."

Amanda put a hand on Naomi's shoulder. "What she means is, you've been hurt before. We just don't want you to make the same mistakes again."

"Or bring that mistake into all of our lives," Miriam added. "You've got to think of the family, not just yourself."

"I'm not being selfish. I'm thinking about all of us. Didn't we just all agree that Gideon is a *gut* worker and that we need the help?"

"I didn't say you're selfish—"

"Don't change the subject. Didn't we just agree we need his help?"

Miriam exhaled. "I guess you could say that."

"I'm not saying it. Amanda and Leah did."

Miriam exhaled again.

"Do I need to remind you of the scripture 'Be not forgetful to entertain strangers'?" Naomi asked.

"You've reminded me plenty," Miriam said.

"Just doing my duty," Naomi said.

Miriam raised her eyebrows. "Interesting that you've never found the need to bring other strangers home before to do your duty."

Naomi snorted.

Leah and Amanda laughed, then cut it off abruptly when Naomi glared at them.

"What is it that you're asking, Naomi?" Miriam said. "Let's just get to the point."

"Oh, *vell*, that's easy. We should invite Gideon to stay after the two weeks are up and David's parents *kumme* back to town. He should move into the spare room where John lived before he married Leah."

"That does make sense, Miriam," Leah said.

Amanda nodded. "He's proved himself so far, and the bishop has vouched for him."

Miriam considered for a moment, then gave a quick, decisive nod. "I'm not going to argue that. I agree. We should give that serious consideration." She swung her eyes to Naomi and gave a sharp look. "As long as he doesn't do anything to lose our trust."

Naomi met her sister's eyes with a steady, confident gaze. "He won't." She clasped her hands together. Everything felt so good and right. The world was falling into place, just as it should. She could not keep the smile off her face. "This is perfect," she murmured. "Just perfect."

Miriam did not look so sure, but she did not disagree.

"You know, he was just telling me how much he's always wanted a farm just like this." Naomi took a deep, cleansing breath. She felt so relaxed and confident now. "His family never had their own farm when he was growing up, you know. So he's been dreaming of having one his whole life. One with a big old farmhouse, an oak tree, a lake—everything that we have here. Isn't that *wunderbar*? It's too much to be a coincidence."

When no one responded, Naomi stopped to study their expressions. Miriam's mouth was set in a tight line. Amanda and Leah were exchanging a quick, concerned glance with one another.

Naomi frowned. "What is it?"

"Naomi, you're right—" Miriam started to say.

"Ha! So you finally see—"

"You're right that it's too much to be a coincidence," Miriam interrupted.

"Exactly! There has to be a reason that—"

Leah cut Naomi off by putting a hand on her arm. "*Ya*. But it might not be the reason you think."

"Or that you want it to be," Amanda added gently.

Naomi looked over at Miriam. She expected her to have that familiar condescending look. But instead, Miriam just looked sad. Naomi put her hands on her hips. "*Oll recht*, what's going on? I can tell that all three of you are thinking the same thing and you're leaving me out, as usual."

Leah gave Naomi's arm a gentle squeeze before letting go. "We're trying to explain it, but I don't think you want to hear."

"*Vell*, try me."

Her sisters all looked at each other. Amanda shook her head and Miriam frowned.

"Come on. Tell me what you're thinking."

Amanda sighed and looked down.

"Isn't it obvious?" Leah asked. Her voice was kind, but that only made Naomi feel worse.

"Stop patronizing me."

"*Oll recht*," Miriam said. "Can't you see that it's too much of a coincidence that Gideon has always wanted a farm just like this one?"

Naomi narrowed her eyes. "Say it out loud. Go on."

Miriam threw up her hands. "He wants the farm. And you're his way to get it."

"He's not using me," Naomi said. But even as she said it, doubt rippled through her. She had been foolish and naive before. Was she being foolish and naive now? Could she trust her own instincts when they had proved wrong in the past?

Leah made eye contact with Miriam and shook her head, just slightly.

Miriam shook her head in return and threw up her hands again.

Leah frowned, then turned her attention to Naomi. "We're not saying that it's your fault or that you've done anything wrong."

"I know that."

Leah nodded. "We're just saying that it seems too…convenient. Gideon comes here and tells you that his dream is to have a farm just like this one."

"And, meanwhile, he's being so charming that you can't help falling for him," Amanda cut in.

"Maybe he is that charming," Naomi said. But the words sounded childish as she said them. "And maybe he happens to share our dreams. He also said he always wanted a family like ours."

Miriam's expression sharpened. "I don't like this. I don't like any of this."

"He's so withdrawn," Amanda said. "It is a little suspicious. He barely speaks."

"What? A few minutes ago, you were arguing that he should stay and help you with the herd! He's a *gut* worker, remember?"

"*Vell*, yeah, but what if he's making a show of being a *gut* worker because he's trying to weasel his way into getting his hands on the farm?"

Naomi stomped her foot. She knew it was immature, but she was too angry to stop herself. This was outrageous. "He is not some criminal mastermind!"

Amanda put up a hand. "You're right. I didn't mean it to

sound as bad as it did. But I do think he's had a hard life. Maybe he's not above getting what he can, even if it's not the honest way of getting it."

"Just because he's had a hard life doesn't mean he's a bad person."

Amanda rubbed her temple. "I didn't say that."

"You may as well have," Naomi said.

"He might not be doing it to hurt you, but if he's using you to get a share of the farm, then it will hurt you, whatever his intentions are."

"I can't believe this. Are you saying that you don't want him to move into the house, after all?"

Her three sisters exchanged glances.

Miriam sighed. "We can't ignore how suspicious it looks. He's been acting sweet on you since the moment he got here. And now we find out he wants the farm. What else are we supposed to think?"

"How about that I'm worth loving? That maybe he actually *is* sweet on me? Ever think of that?"

"*Ach*, Naomi." Miriam squeezed he eyes shut for a moment, before opening them again. "I'm sorry. Of course you're worth loving. It's just that…" She adjusted her apron and straightened the sleeve of her blue dress. She refused to look Naomi in the eye. "He might not be the one who is going to give you that love."

"You don't know that."

"This isn't a fairy tale, Naomi." Miriam's expression sharpened. "Prince Charming doesn't just show up on your doorstep."

"Maybe he does!" Naomi shouted. "Just because you don't believe in love doesn't mean it isn't real!" Naomi swung her attention to Leah and Amanda. "And you two have no right to talk." She pointed her finger at them. "Especially you, Leah. John wasn't even Amish when you fell for him."

"That was different."

Naomi popped her hands onto her hips. "Oh really? How?"

Leah swallowed hard. "Because I wasn't looking to fall in love. I didn't want to."

"What are you saying? That I've made this all up in my head?"

Leah's eyes widened. "Uh…" She glanced at Miriam.

Miriam sighed. "Not that you've made it up…exactly. But that you're easily persuaded. If you expect to see something, if you want to see it, you'll find it everywhere."

"It's not like that."

"I hope you're right." Miriam's voice sounded distant and sad. She looked tired.

"*Nee*, you don't. You want to prove to everyone that love isn't real. Otherwise, you'll have to face the fact that you made a terrible mistake when you lost your chance for it."

Miriam inhaled. Her face tightened. "You'd do well to learn from my past, instead of repeating it."

"I'm not you, Miriam. And this has nothing to do with your past."

Miriam took a steadying breath.

Naomi was always surprised at how calm her sister could remain, even when under the most intense emotions. It didn't seem natural, not to her at least. She could never hide how she really felt.

"You're right. This has nothing to do with my past. And, you'll remember, I never said it did."

Naomi opened her mouth to argue but Miriam shot her a look that could curdle milk.

"Regardless of what happened to me, there are bad men

out there, who don't have *gut* intentions, who want to get what they can from you and walk away."

"Or stay for the wrong reasons, if that's what benefits them," Amanda added.

"You mean if they get a farm out of it?" Naomi asked. She was trying to show them how ludicrous that was, but instead they all nodded.

"*Ya*. That's exactly what we mean," Leah said.

"I can't believe you all," Naomi said. She turned and marched toward the door. She had heard enough.

"I don't want you to learn the hard way," Miriam said.

Naomi did not turn around. She wanted to shout that love was real and that was what she and Gideon had. But that confidence was wilting like a flower left too long without water. Her sisters had managed to plant doubt in her heart.

As she stormed out the door and into the bright morning sunlight, Naomi had no idea what to do or what to think. She had never felt so frustrated or confused.

Chapter Ten

Gideon could feel the tension. It followed him through the farmhouse, across the farmyard, and into the goat shed like a shadow. Whenever he ran into one of the Stoltzfus sisters that morning, their conversation stopped abruptly and their eyes darted from one to another, refusing to meet him in the eye.

At lunch, the family ate on the picnic tables beneath the old oak tree. The meal would have been lovely with big, billowing clouds overhead and sunlight streaming through the oak leaves. A soft breeze carried the scent of wildflowers and Ollie's distant barks as he watched over the goats in the high pasture. But the awkward silence took away from the peaceful atmosphere.

Even Naomi seemed off-kilter. She kept frowning, as if she were thinking about something, while nibbling an ear of corn. Gideon was pretty sure he knew what had happened. Naomi had tried to stand up for him. The men must not have heard about the conflict yet, because they were devouring the stack of ham sandwiches as if they had not eaten in days.

John sighed, pushed his plate away, and patted his belly. "*Vell*, I can't fit another bite."

Leah smiled. "You sure about that? Because we have cherry pie." She pulled a red-checkered dish towel off of a pie tin to reveal a golden, flaky crust crisscrossed over deep red filling.

John grinned. "There's always room for dessert."

"Especially when you're six-four," David said as he reached for the pie before John could grab it. "You may be bigger, but I'm faster."

Everyone at the table laughed. Abby noticed the noise and looked up from where she and Caleb lay on a blanket in the shade of the oak tree. She gave a gummy smile and cooed. Caleb babbled and reached for his rattle. The border collies lounged in the shade beside the babies, ears pricked and alert, waiting for someone to throw them a bite of ham.

"Here you go," Gideon whispered and slipped each dog a slice of ham from his sandwich. Their tails thumped against the ground as they gobbled it down, then looked up at him with dark brown eyes, hoping for more.

Gideon could almost relax. He was surrounded by a family—not his, but a family nonetheless—who loved each other, despite their differences and disagreements. They were lively and fun and he could imagine being a part of that easy camaraderie.

Except he was not welcome here. He was not a part of it and never would be. The quick, guarded glances from the Stoltzfus sisters made that much clear. So did their silence. He sensed that they were watching him, sizing him up, waiting for him to make a mistake. Was he just being paranoid and overly sensitive? He hoped so, but if Naomi did speak to her sisters about his staying, then he was definitely not being paranoid. They simply did not want him here.

Gideon looked over at Naomi. She sat across from him, picking at her sandwich. "You want me to grab you some pie before John eats it all?" he asked.

John chuckled. “Better get it fast.” He was already on his second slice.

“Naomi?” She was miles away and startled when Gideon said her name.

Her eyes jerked up from her plate to meet his. “Huh?”

“You want some pie?”

“Oh.” She frowned. “Um, no thanks. I’m full.”

“You’ve barely eaten.”

“I guess I’m just not very hungry today.”

Now it was Gideon’s turn to frown. He didn’t like seeing her upset. He hoped he wasn’t the cause of it. Then he remembered that he shouldn’t frown so much. It put people off, even though he wasn’t being unfriendly. It was just the expression he made when he was feeling serious or concerned—which happened to be most of the time. No wonder the Stoltzfus family was suspicious of him. He had done a lousy job of impressing them. If only he could be more like Benjamin, with his warm jokes and quick grin. Or like David and John, who found meaningful ways to contribute to the family business. John always had a construction project going and David was often out with the herd, alongside Amanda. No wonder they seemed so at ease and at home. They were needed and appreciated.

But not Gideon. He was easily replaceable. He was a farmhand with no special skills. He knew nothing about goats and only the basics when it came to construction. He could do basic handyman repairs, but that was about it. Sure, he was great at manual labor, but lots of men could do that. What did he have to offer Stoneybrook Farm? More importantly, what did he have to offer Naomi? So far, it seemed like all he had done was make her life worse. Or more complicated, at least. He never should have opened up to her about his dreams.

And yet he had done it anyway. Now, he would surely pay the price.

After lunch, Gideon went to work mucking out the goat pen. The sun grew hot on his shoulders and sweat beaded across his forehead. He took off his straw hat, wiped his brow, and kept working. Maybe someone would notice and see that he had a good heart and good intentions. No one did, of course.

After he finished with the goat pen, he took care of the horses' stalls in the barn, then cleared some brush out of the back pasture. After that, he chopped firewood and stacked it on the enclosed back porch. By the time evening came around, his arms ached and stray bits of straw clung to his blue work shirt. And he still had not done anything that would impress anyone in the Stoltzfus family. They would not think, *Hey, he sure did chop a lot of firewood. We should invite him to stay.* No, just about anyone could chop and stack firewood. He needed to do something that would get their attention and make him valuable to the farm. Then maybe, just maybe, he would be welcome here.

And, more importantly, he would have something to offer Naomi. If he had something to offer her, he might be able to court her.

No. He was getting ahead of himself. It had been painfully clear at lunch that day that he was not one of them. Why would Naomi accept him as a suitor? Yes, she had said that she liked him. And they had had that remarkable, golden moment beneath the stars, when he sensed that there was more than friendship between them. But that didn't mean it could happen practically, in the real world.

In the real world, women like Naomi had to think about what their families thought and about what a husband could bring to the table. He had nothing to bring but himself. And clearly, that was not enough. It never had been for anyone else, so how could it be now?

Unless he could think of something that he *could* offer. It wouldn't be much, whatever it was, but maybe it could be a start.

Now all he had to do was think of something.

Naomi wished that she didn't care what her sisters thought. She did not want to want their approval. But she did. She could not help it. And she was worried that they might be right. What if she couldn't trust her own instincts? What if she needed to listen to their perspective? She didn't want to believe that, but the thought nibbled away at her, like a hungry mouse gnawing down a wedge of cheese. Pretty soon, she felt like she had been nibbled to pieces. She had to stop this. She had to trust herself.

But what if she was wrong?

Naomi frowned and lifted the mop bucket. Water sloshed over the sides and washed over her bare feet. She gasped and stepped back fast, which made the water slosh over again. This time, the spray hit her up to her knees. Nothing was going right today. Naomi sighed as she dragged the bucket outside, the wet fabric of her dress clinging to her legs. She hauled the bucket over the porch railing, leaned over, and dumped it out.

She could not pull her thoughts from Gideon and stood staring at the mud puddle she had just made. A hen clucked and strutted through the puddle with her head held high as if she owned the farm. Naomi smiled. The world was such a big, beautiful place, full of happy chickens, cute babies, and beautiful sunsets. If only she could solve the problem with Gideon, then everything would be perfect.

She sighed and leaned against the railing. But how could

she know if he was being genuine or not? How could anyone ever know what someone else was thinking or feeling?

"Hey, Naomi."

Naomi's attention shot up at the sound of Gideon's voice. She saw him jogging across the farmyard. He jumped the puddle, rounded the corner of the porch, and trotted up the steps. "I've been thinking."

Naomi's brow creased. She couldn't tell if this were good or bad. "About what?"

"I have an idea." He scratched his arm and looked out over the yard. The hen stopped pecking the earth to look back at him. "If you don't mind taking a minute to hear it." He glanced at the empty bucket in her hand. "I guess you're busy."

"*Nee*. I can't go back inside for a little while. I mopped myself into a corner—or out the door, actually. I have to wait for it to dry." Naomi realized that she should be embarrassed. Grown women were supposed to know how to mop a floor without making silly mistakes. They were not supposed to be so busy daydreaming that they forgot what they were doing.

Gideon laughed. "That's what I like about you, Naomi. Always dreaming."

"You like that?"

Gideon's smile looked so genuine. Could this all be an act to sweep her off her feet and push his way into owning a share of Stoneybrook Farm? Surely not. You know a tree by its fruits. And Gideon's fruits were good. He was kind to animals and children. He was gentle and thoughtful. He was always ready to help anyone who needed it. How could he be faking all of that? Some men did, she supposed. But surely not Gideon. He would have to be very, very good at deceit. Wouldn't he have slipped up by now? Wouldn't his true nature start to show through the cracks?

Of course, her sisters would say that she simply had not been around him long enough to see those cracks forming. She needed to give it more time. But she did not want to give it more time. She wanted to hold his hand now. She wanted to ride in the courting buggy under the stars and talk all night. She wanted to hear his thoughts and dreams and share hers in return. She wanted all the things that she had hoped and planned for since she had read her first Amish romance novel and realized that love was real and she could find it one day.

But just because she wanted something didn't make it right or good. She might have daydreamed herself into a disaster.

"Would you like to sit down for a minute? I mean, if you have time. If you—" Gideon frowned and looked down "—want to."

Naomi was beginning to recognize that frown. She was pretty sure that it meant that he was nervous or worried. She felt all her caution dissolving. "Of course I want to."

"You've probably been on your feet all day."

"Same as you."

"It's *gut*, honest work."

Naomi nodded as she padded to the row of white rocking chairs. The wooden floorboards felt rough and cool against her bare feet. "Do you want a glass of lemonade? I like to sit out here and have one every afternoon. Sometimes Miriam says I waste too much time, but it makes me happy. It gives me a chance to sit and appreciate all of *Gott*'s creations." A butterfly flitted past on brilliant purple wings. "See what I mean? You notice things like that when you sit for a minute and just…do nothing."

"I see what you mean. And that lemonade sounds nice, but isn't the floor wet?"

Naomi hit her forehead with the heel of her hand. "*Recht.* I already forgot." She shrugged and dropped into a chair. "*Vell*, the view is just as nice without the lemonade."

"That's true." Gideon settled into the rocker beside Naomi and studied the sweeping hillside. The pasture sloped downward into the Yoder land, into the gleaming yellow sunflower field and the distant, shimmering lake. A family of ducks paddled in circles, dipping their heads underwater, then popping up again.

The porch creaked as their rockers went back and forth. Naomi snuck a glance at Gideon, then looked back out over the land again. Gideon took off his straw hat and held it in his hands. "I, uh, guess you're waiting for me to say something. I'm not so *gut* with words, you know."

"I think you're just fine with them. Some people think that talking a lot means you must have important things to say. I never thought that."

Gideon smiled. "Me either."

Naomi was curious about what Gideon had to say, but she didn't mind sitting and rocking for a while. The breeze was warm, but the shade from the porch's roof made the temperature feel just right. A bee buzzed in the distance and one of the babies laughed from the side yard, followed by the murmur of voices. It was a nice afternoon for sitting and doing nothing before going back to work.

"So," Gideon said after a while. "I was thinking maybe I could help out more around here."

"But you've been working all day. I saw the goat shed this afternoon. It's spick-and-span."

Gideon held his straw hat in his lap and picked at the edge of the brim as he rocked. "*Vell*, I'm glad to hear that. But I was thinking I could do more." He turned to look at her. "I want to give back more. You know, really contribute something." He frowned and turned back to face the yard. His chair kept creaking as he rocked back and forth.

Was he trying to impress her? Her sisters? All of them? Was this his way of fooling her into thinking that he had good intentions? That didn't feel right. She wasn't a suspicious person. It just didn't come naturally. She wasn't sure how hard she should push herself to be that way. Maybe she just needed to try harder not to trust him.

"I was thinking about an ad I saw in *The Budget* the other day," Gideon said. "It was for a livestock auction near here. I think it was called Byler Brothers' Livestock Market. They need to sell some farm animals that have been neglected. They aren't worth much because they're malnourished. I guess I haven't been able to stop thinking about it because if they don't sell, they'll be going to the slaughterhouse."

"How awful," Naomi said.

"I agree. But, of course, it wouldn't be practical to buy them."

Naomi laughed. "Now you sound like Miriam."

Gideon smiled, but did not laugh. There was a seriousness behind his eyes. "So, I was thinking about how I could do more for Stoneybrook Farm, and I was thinking about those animals, and then it hit me."

Naomi straightened up. "What?"

Gideon glanced at her, then looked away again. He shifted in his seat. "It's a silly idea—"

"I doubt it."

Gideon's smile widened a little. "The family's been growing, ain't so? Leah and Amanda got married not too long ago. Benjamin too. And that added babies *and* in-laws."

"*Ya.* It's a full house."

"That's a lot of mouths to feed. So I figure we—I mean you all—could use another income stream."

"Sure. That's always a *gut* thing."

Gideon took a deep breath, turned to her, and grinned. "We could start a petting zoo."

"A petting zoo?"

"You don't like the idea?"

"Are you kidding? I love it!" Naomi clapped her hands together. "It's perfect!"

Gideon beamed. "You really think so?"

"*Ya*. Do you think there's a pig for sale at that auction? I always wanted a pig. They're the cutest. But don't tell Amanda I said that—she thinks goats are the cutest." Naomi stopped herself. "I'm talking too much, aren't I?"

Gideon's eyes were shining. "Not at all. I like hearing what you have to say."

Suddenly, Naomi was at a loss for words. No one had ever wanted to hear her prattle on before.

"I like pigs too," Gideon said. "I like the way they snort. It's cute."

"Exactly!" Naomi snorted like a pig.

Then Gideon snorted in return.

They both laughed, then they both snorted again. Next thing Naomi knew, they were laughing so hard that her belly ached and she was wiping tears from her eyes. This connection felt too genuine to be faked. Something never felt quite right with the men who had courted her before. Sure, they were charming and thoughtful on the surface, but after spending time with them, the cracks started to show.

But with Gideon there weren't any red flags. Okay, there was his arrest record. She shouldn't totally discount that. But his actions now were what mattered. And there were no quick, angry glances or hints that he was just looking to use her. Well, unless her sisters were right about the farm. He did want a farm just like this one.

But she could see the genuine connection, honesty, gentleness, selflessness. His actions were considerate and thoughtful. Those were not qualities that her other suitors had had. They turned on the charm, but they could not completely hide who they were. She had not been able to see it right away because she had not understood that someone would put up a false front to get their way. But now that she had been burned twice, Naomi was sure she could recognize it.

And she did not see it in Gideon.

"I was afraid you might think it was silly, or, I don't know..." Gideon shrugged. "Childish? It isn't very manly to get emotional over animals."

"Are you kidding me? If that's not manly then I don't know what is. Real men aren't afraid to feel their emotions. Everyone has them, you know. It seems pretty silly to me to pretend otherwise. It's how *Gott* made us, ain't so?"

Gideon smiled. "*Vell*, when you put it that way..."

Naomi smiled back as they gazed into one another's eyes. She drifted into the moment for a few beats too long. She knew that she was being obvious about her feelings, staring at him like that, but his eyes were so soft and warm, so inviting.

Belinda's honking pulled her out of the moment. She looked over to see the goose waddling to the edge of the fence. She flapped her wings a few times, pushed out her long neck, and honked again. Belinda could see danger when Naomi couldn't. Naomi glanced back at Gideon and swallowed hard. She was so sure that she had the right idea about him. But what if there was danger lurking in the shadows, beyond what she could see?

Naomi pushed the fear aside. She had no evidence for it in his actions, just her sisters' concerns. "How will we get people to come to the petting zoo?"

Gideon nodded. "I've been thinking about that. We get a pretty *gut* stream of traffic coming off the highway to buy fresh goat milk."

"And the goat milk soap that Benjamin and Emma make," Naomi added. The little start-up that had helped spark their romance was thriving now.

"*Recht*," Gideon said. "We could make a bigger sign and add the petting zoo to it. People will stop just to see the animals, then buy goat milk and soap while they're here. We can also sell animal feed for them to hand out."

"Oh, right. I've seen those little machines before at petting zoos. The ones where you put in the money and turn the dial. Or sometimes, they sell the feed in plastic cups."

"I've been to one where they sell baby bottles full of milk and you can feed the baby goats from it."

"That's so cute," Naomi said.

"It was." Gideon chuckled. "Hopefully the tourists will think so too."

"Oh, they'll love it. I bet we'll get a lot more people in here. And word of mouth will spread fast. I'll see if we can get the information added to some of the Lancaster County tourism brochures. They already have Stoneybrook Farm listed as a *gut* place to buy farm-fresh products. But this will turn us into a tourist attraction on top of that." Naomi gave a decisive nod. "This could be lucrative."

"Even if it works more as a way to draw more people to the farm than a way to make money directly."

"Exactly." Naomi tapped a finger against her chin. "But we could play around with it, maybe charge people a few dollars to pet the animals. That could add up fast."

"Sure could." Gideon paused, then put a hand on Naomi's arm. "I'm glad you like the idea." He pulled his hand away and looked down. His cheeks reddened and Naomi knew that he was embarrassed to have shown his excitement. He might be afraid that he crossed a line by touching her elbow. But she was glad he had. She felt a thrill of excitement race down her spine. Maybe, just maybe, everything would work out, after all.

But first, she would have to be sure that Gideon was as genuine as she hoped he was. And she would have to convince her sisters to accept him and his new idea.

Chapter Eleven

Gideon felt a huge relief that Naomi believed in his idea. For the first time in as long as he could remember, he felt like he had a true friend who really believed in him. But he didn't want to let himself get carried away. And he certainly didn't want to tell her sisters right away. He would rather prove himself first. But Naomi wanted to get it over with. He could tell that she was nervous about gaining their approval, which only made him more nervous. They were sure to criticize his plan. If for no other reason than because it would give him a reason to stay at Stoneybrook Farm.

But he was no coward. He might hate confrontation, but he would face it when he needed to. And, if he could make this petting zoo plan work, it could lead to a permanent home and, more importantly, a way to stay close to Naomi.

They found Miriam and Leah hanging a quilt on the clothesline in the backyard. Abby lay on a blanket in the grass, kicking her feet and babbling. "Where's everyone else?" Naomi asked.

"Amanda and David are in the south pasture with the goats. Katie's planning on helping them up there when she gets home from school. John's in the barn, I think." Miriam stood on her tiptoes to throw the wet, heavy fabric over the line. Gideon swooped in and pulled it into place. He was average height, but Miriam and Amanda were short—he guessed they couldn't be much taller than five feet—so he was tall in comparison. Amanda handed him a clothespin, stepped back, and stretched her back. "*Danki*," she said.

Miriam stepped back too, but her expression was more guarded than Amanda's. "You look like you have something to say, Naomi."

"Gideon has an idea."

Miriam's expression did not soften. Gideon wished that Naomi had said it was her idea. Her family would be more likely to listen, then. He didn't care about getting credit or attention. He just wanted to be able to stay at Stoneybrook Farm. Of course, that meant they had to recognize that he was the one behind the plan, so they would value him. Gideon's jaw tightened. He didn't like being the center of attention, even if it was for a good cause. Especially when Miriam was staring him down as if he were plotting a devious mission. The familiar wave of shame crept over him. How many times had people looked at him like that, with narrowed eyes full of judgment?

"It's a really *gut* one," Naomi said.

Miriam sighed. "*Oll recht*. Let's hear it."

"Benjamin should hear it too," Naomi said. "Where is he? He'll love it."

"He was just here…" Amanda looked around.

The door to the enclosed back porch swung open and Benjamin popped out, cradling Caleb in his arms. Emma trailed behind him with a mug of coffee in her hand. "I was just giving Emma a break," Benjamin said.

Gideon was relieved to see them. Benjamin and Emma were fun-loving and supportive. He felt confident that they would back him. More importantly, he knew that they had fallen in love after Caleb's *Englischer* father abandoned

Emma during a disastrous *rumspringa*. Neither of them judged people for past mistakes.

"I'll go get John," Leah said, then hitched up the skirt of her dress and jogged across the backyard, around the house, and out of sight.

Gideon felt like everyone was waiting for him to speak. But Leah was gone, so he thought he ought to hold off. But waiting felt too awkward. The seconds ticked past as he contemplated what to do. A bee buzzed past his face, then darted to a patch of clover in the grass. The sun looked bright against the white flowers and green leaves. "Weather's nice today," he murmured, then immediately regretted it. He was terrible at small talk.

Gideon exhaled as Leah and John bounded around the corner. "Okay," Leah said, slightly out of breath, "tell us. We can catch David and Amanda up when they come in for supper."

Everyone's eyes swung to Gideon. Suddenly, his idea didn't seem so good anymore. What if they laughed? What if they thought it was silly? Worse, what if they shut the idea down and he lost his chance to contribute and stay on the farm?

Naomi nudged him in the ribs with her elbow. He cleared his throat. "*Vell*, I was thinking that Stoneybrook Farm could use another income stream. You know, since the family's been growing so fast lately." He felt a hot flush of nervous embarrassment creep up his spine. "You know, with the new in-laws and babies. I mean, John and Emma and—"

"We know what you mean," Miriam said. "Go on and tell us your idea."

Gideon's embarrassment intensified. The more he tried to explain himself, the more muddled he sounded. "Uh, *recht*. So, I've been thinking about ways to bring in more money to the farm."

Miriam stared up at him in a way that reminded him of his teacher back at the one-room schoolhouse. She could make him feel far smaller than her with just one look.

Gideon kept going. “I think we—I mean you all—should have a petting zoo. It would attract more tourists, who would buy more products when they come here, and they would pay to pet and feed the animals.”

“Sounds like a *gut* idea to me,” Benjamin said. Caleb cooed in his arms and Benjamin grinned down at his stepson. “You think so too, huh?” Caleb cooed again. “*Vell*, looks like it’s decided, then.”

Everyone but Miriam laughed. “Can’t argue that,” Emma said.

But Miriam looked like she definitely could.

“They’re auctioning off some neglected farm animals at Byler Brothers’ Livestock Market,” Naomi said. “They’re going to be cheap. Probably no more than the cost to haul them away. It’s a great investment.”

“And we’ll be saving them from the slaughterhouse,” Gideon added. “I think they deserve a second chance.”

Miriam’s expression shifted as she studied him and Gideon wondered what she was thinking. It looked like she might be softening toward him, just a little.

“I saw something about that in *The Budget*,” Benjamin said. “I remember thinking that I wished there was something we could do.”

“Oh *recht*, you told me about that,” Emma said. “The *Englischer* who owned the animals moved here from Philadelphia and didn’t realize what he was getting into. He didn’t know how much time and money it would take.”

“That happens sometimes,” Leah said. “Farming isn’t as easy as city folk think.”

John chuckled. “Sure isn’t. But it’s worth the effort.” He

pulled Leah closer and she rested her cheek against his shoulder. They both smiled and Gideon could not help but feel a pang of loneliness. He wanted to show his affection to Naomi in a casual move like that. He wanted to pull her closer, in front of everyone, without fear of what they might think. But he was getting ahead of himself. He and Naomi weren't even courting. Sure, they had admitted that they liked one another—but that did not mean that she wanted it to turn into a courtship. Liking someone did not mean you wanted something more.

"Great!" Naomi beamed. "Gideon and I will go to the auction—"

"Leah needs to run the numbers first, to make sure we can afford to—" Miriam cut in before being interrupted by Leah.

"*Ya*, I'll do it right away. But I'm ninety-nine percent sure it will be a *gut* investment."

"*Vell*, make it one hundred percent," Miriam said. "Anyone else have any other...concerns?"

"Nope." Benjamin grinned at Caleb and he flashed a big, gummy smile in return.

"I love the idea, Gideon," Emma said.

"Even you have to admit it's a *gut* idea," Naomi said to Miriam.

Miriam frowned. "It does sound like a *gut* way to attract more people and make more sales."

Naomi laughed. "Then don't look so unhappy about it."

Miriam's frown deepened. "I'm not. I'm just thinking."

Gideon was sure he knew what she was thinking—she was worried that this plan would enable him to stay. That was the point, of course, but he wished she had not caught on. Nothing slipped past Miriam though. At least it was a good idea. And Miriam was clearly a good businesswoman. She would not pass up a chance to help Stoneybrook Farm increase profits. Even if that complicated things later on. And it would. Because he was that complication. He intended to stay, even if she did not want him here. He would no longer slink away in shame, allowing others to determine his life path. He would stand strong and do what he knew was right.

He would fight for a chance to win over Naomi.

And that fight, ironically, would begin with adopting a menagerie of abandoned animals. He was more than ready. And, judging by Naomi's expression, so was she. He longed to take her hand and squeeze it to signal that they were together on this. Instead, he settled for a moment of eye contact and shared smiles. He could feel the connection and excitement spark between them. And for the first time, he didn't care who else noticed.

Naomi was so happy that she felt like her heart might burst. She was by Gideon's side, surrounded by adorable animals, ready to launch a new adventure. Her concerns about Gideon were still there, somewhere, but they felt dim and far away. It was hard to keep reminding herself to worry about his intentions when she was this excited.

Gideon shifted his feet as they sat on the metal bleachers of the auction house, waiting for their lot of animals to come up for bid. He smiled whenever their eyes met, but she could sense his nervousness. She figured that he felt pressured to prove himself, since this was his idea. And it was a pretty outlandish idea. But that was why she liked him so much. He was the type of man to care about neglected animals. He was the type of man to be gentle and kind enough that those animals would respond to him. He was not the type of man to sweep a woman off her feet just to take her farm.

Was he?

Naomi glanced at Gideon again. He was leaning forward,

eyes alert, elbows braced over his knees, as he watched the auctioneer. He looked too unsure, too nervous to be plotting some evil scheme. It was getting harder and harder to hold on to the doubt. If Gideon were trying to trick her into falling for him, then he was the best actor on the planet.

Of course, he might be a very talented actor. All this could be an elaborate ruse…

Naomi furrowed her brow and squared her shoulders. She had to be tough. She would watch him closely. She would try not to let herself jump to conclusions—even though it was hard not to, when he looked at her with those rich blue eyes. She needed to make a decision based on his actions, not on the things he said or the way he made her heart leap.

The more she thought about it, the more confident Naomi became. She was not basing her decisions on sweet nothings whispered in her ear. She was basing it on how he treated her and how he treated others. That was a pretty surefire measuring stick, it seemed to her. He had not even lost his patience with Miriam, even though she must have offended him. He had never questioned her authority or spoken ill of her behind her back. He had always treated her with respect. Naomi figured that the way a man treated a woman in a position of authority said a lot about him.

"Lot number 496," the auctioneer shouted into the microphone. "Lot number 496 is open for bids."

Naomi jerked her attention back to the auction ring, where a handful of men were leading an odd assortment of skinny animals. There were a few sheep with hollow eyes and dirty wool coats that were full of burs. A small donkey gazed up at the crowd with big black eyes. Three rabbits huddled in a hutch, trembling at the noise inside the big open room filled with bleachers of Amish and *Englischers*. A camel with long legs and a patchy coat lumbered into the ring.

Naomi gasped. “A camel!”

Gideon’s eyes widened. He glanced at her, then back at the ring. “We may be getting more than we bargained for.”

The camel looked at the crowd through long black eyelashes, then tugged at the rope the auction worker was holding. The man held firm and the camel bellowed.

“I’ve never seen a camel up close before,” Gideon said. “I don’t know how to take care of one.”

“We can learn. Besides, I bet you’ll be a natural. Animals love you.”

Gideon’s brow creased. “I don’t want to buy him if we can’t take *gut* care of him. He deserves a *gut* home.”

“But what if no one else wants to give him a home?” Naomi asked. “What will happen then?”

Gideon rubbed his jaw. “I don’t know. Do they send camels to the slaughterhouse?”

“I don’t know either.”

“*Vell*, whatever it is it can’t be *gut*.” Gideon shook his head. “It’s going to take a lot of love and care to get those animals back in good health.”

“*Gut* thing we have plenty of love to give.” Naomi regretted the words as soon as she said them. Did it sound like she was hinting that they had love for each other? She had meant that there was plenty of love at Stoneybrook Farm to go around. But just mentioning the word *love* around Gideon made her feel exposed. She stuck her hand into the air and shouted out a low number. It had been instinct, to distract herself from embarrassment. Had she acted too soon?

But Gideon just smiled and nodded. “Go for it,” he said.

Suddenly, Naomi felt like they were together in some harebrained scheme that only they could truly understand. And, the truth was, they were. The rest of the family had agreed to go along with it, including Amanda and David—as long as it didn't take away from caring for the goats. But none of them understood the need for it like Naomi and Gideon did. This could be the beginning of something big, something that brought them together for good.

Naomi waited for someone else to throw up their hand and shout out a number.

"Do-we-have-another-bid-another-bid-from-anyone?" the auctioneer shouted out in his fast, singsong voice. "Another-bid-anyone?" He glanced around the room. Amish men in black felt hats and *Englischers* in cowboy hats and jeans stared back. No one raised their hand.

Gideon and Naomi exchanged a quick, excited glance.

"Going-going-gone! Sold-to-the-woman-in-the-purple-dress!"

Gideon stood up. "Let's go meet our new friends."

He helped her navigate across the crowded bleachers. A young boy wearing his Sunday best spilled popcorn on the floor as he scooted aside to let them pass. A woman wearing a white *kapp* and apron touched Naomi's arm when she squeezed by. "That was a *gut* thing you did. But I hope you can manage them all."

Naomi felt her first twinge of apprehension. "I hope so too."

By the time they reached the ring, the men were already leading the animals to a truck parked outside. Wood shavings crunched beneath Naomi's black athletic shoes as she followed them out of the big sheet metal building and into the bright sunlight. A third man appeared with a fat pink pig and began to herd her into the back of the trailer. The animal's generous belly swayed beneath her as she walked.

Naomi clapped her hands together. "A pig?"

The man beside the pig stopped and straightened up. He scratched his beard. "Uh, *ya*. We couldn't get her to go into the ring. But she's part of the lot. Did you read the details before you bid?"

"Nee."

"You should have gotten a flyer when you registered to bid."

Naomi remembered crumpling up a sheet of paper in her hand as she wandered past the concession stand and the pens of livestock. "I didn't think to read it."

The man sighed. "*Vell*, we can send her to the slaughterhouse if you don't want to take her with the rest."

"Are you kidding? I've always wanted a pig!"

The man's eyebrows rose. "Is that so?"

"It certain sure is. Does she have a name?"

"Um, she's a pig. I don't think…"

Naomi turned to Gideon. "Let's name her Little Miss Cutie. Because she's so cute."

Gideon laughed. "If you call that cute."

Naomi studied the beady black eyes, wrinkled face, and wet snout. "I do."

Gideon laughed again.

The man in the trailer shook his head. "*Vell*, let's get the rest of them loaded."

The sheep trotted up the ramp and into the trailer bed without a struggle. But the camel pulled against the rope and bellowed. His knobby knees folded and he collapsed to the ground.

Naomi inhaled. "Is he too sick to stand up?"

One of the men laughed. "*Nee*. He's just too stubborn. He does what he wants to do. Camels are like that." The man shook his head. "Just wait until he's full-grown. Then you'll really have your hands full."

"You mean he's still a baby?"

The man scratched his head. "I'd say he's more of a teenager." He chuckled. "And he acts like one."

Another man tugged on the donkey's lead. It looked at the camel, then at the ramp, back to the camel again, gave a loud heehaw, and stood its ground. The auction worker shook his head. "We'll never get her loaded up now." He pulled at the donkey's lead, but she planted her hooves in the dirt and heehawed, flashing oversize yellow teeth.

The other auction worker sighed, took off his straw hat, and wiped his forehead.

Gideon eased toward the donkey. "Let me try."

"If you get one on board, the other will follow. These two are best friends. Strangest thing I ever saw."

"That's so sweet." Naomi knew they had done the right thing to take the whole lot. It would have been terrible to separate two best friends.

One of the men laughed. "It's not so sweet when they both get it in their heads not to budge."

"That's okay. Gideon can handle it. Right, Gideon?"

Gideon frowned. "I can try."

Naomi tried to stop herself, but she could not push down the emotion swelling within her. She and Gideon might be in over their heads with this, but she believed in Gideon. She could not help herself. Maybe Miriam was right and Naomi just couldn't stop herself from falling in love.

The thing was, she didn't want to stop it. It felt too wonderful—even if she was putting herself in danger.

Chapter Twelve

Gideon can handle it. Naomi believed in him. That was huge. Had anyone since his parents ever truly believed in him? But the problem was that he had to prove that he deserved it. And not just right now, in this moment, but over the next days and weeks, for however long he was able to stay by her side.

Gideon could not believe what he had done. He could not possibly manage this strange mix of needy animals. He was sure to fail. Starting right now, in front of everyone.

Naomi nodded at him. Her eyes were shining with trust and excitement. He could not let her down. Well, he would just have to do his best and hope it was good enough.

The camel bellowed and the donkey responded with an ear-splitting heehaw. Gideon took a deep breath and eased forward. "Hey there," he whispered. "Don't want to get in the trailer, huh?" He paused where he was and let them get used to him before easing forward another step. "I don't blame you. Seems like you've been through a lot." He took another slow step forward. "But that's over now. We're going to take *gut* care of you."

The man holding the rope started to hand it to Gideon. But Gideon shook his head. "Just let it go." He didn't want the camel to get the wrong idea about him.

"You sure?" The man looked at him like he was making a very bad decision.

"*Ya*. It's okay."

The man shrugged and dropped the rope.

"Do they have names?" Gideon asked.

"The camel's called Solomon. Answers to Sol, when he feels like it." The man motioned to the donkey. "And her name is Peanut."

"Sol and Peanut. Got it."

Sol chewed his cud in a lazy, sideways motion and gazed up at him through long eyelashes. He did not look like he would get up anytime soon.

Gideon slowly lowered himself to the ground about an arm's length from the camel. "I guess we're going to sit for a while," he murmured. "That's just fine with me. It's been a long day."

Sol swung his head around to watch him.

Peanut pushed her muzzle forward, toward Gideon, and brayed.

"They don't know what to think," Naomi said.

Gideon smiled to himself. He felt more comfortable around animals than people. They were straightforward and honest. If you treated them well, they treated you well. If you showed that you had good intentions, they trusted you.

Sol kept chewing his cud and studying Gideon.

Gideon stretched out his legs, leaned back onto his palms, and closed his eyes. The sunlight felt warm on his face.

"Uh, how long is this going to take?" one of the auction workers asked. "We've got more trailers to load."

Gideon didn't open his eyes. "As long as it takes."

He heard them shifting their feet and whispering. He hoped that Naomi didn't think that he was as strange as they did. But he knew that earning an animal's trust took time. You had to put them at ease first.

One of the men cleared his throat. "We're going to head back inside and leave it to you. Let us know if you need any help."

Gideon opened his eyes and gave a quick, polite nod. "Sure thing. *Danki* for the help."

He could hear them whispering as they walked back inside the auction house.

Naomi stepped closer. "Can I sit down with you?" she whispered as she glanced from the donkey to the camel.

"*Ya*. Just don't make any loud noises or sudden movements."

"Oll recht."

It felt good when she eased down beside him. When her elbow rested against his, it warmed his arm more than the sun did. "I hope you don't mind waiting."

"*Nee*. It's nice here."

Gideon chuckled. "In the dirt, out back beside the rental trailers?"

Naomi smiled. "With you—" Her smile dropped. "I mean with you and the animals. It's nice and sunny. I like having time to sit and do nothing."

The crowd's shouts and the auctioneer's voice rumbled through the sheet metal walls, but Gideon felt like he and Naomi were the only people in the world. He hoped that she had corrected herself because she wanted to be here with him, but was afraid to admit it.

Or else, she realized that she had come off the wrong way. She might be trying to keep her distance. After all, her siblings seemed very persuasive. She might be here because she loved animals, not because she loved him.

He had not meant to think about love. They had said they

liked each other. That was a big deal, but it didn't mean anything. Schoolchildren liked each other. Friends liked each other. He wanted something more than like. But only if she did too.

And he wasn't sure that she did. She was so sweet and eager to please. That meant that he could easily misinterpret her. He would not assume that she wanted a friendship to become a courtship. Especially with a drifter like him, with nothing to offer.

"Do you think it's working?" Naomi whispered.

Gideon had almost forgotten what he was doing. He had gotten too caught up in his thoughts of Naomi, and how close she was sitting beside him. "I hope so." He shifted his weight off his hands, reached inside his black coat, and pulled out a small plastic baggie of sliced apples. "And I brought a little help." He pulled open the baggie and pulled out a slice. "Want one, Sol?"

The camel yawned, then snorted.

Peanut took a step closer, dragging her rope behind her. "Ease over real slow and get a hold of her lead," Gideon whispered. He held the apple slice up while Naomi scooted behind him, toward the rope. The donkey brayed, took another step forward, then hesitated. Gideon knew how to be patient. He was always waiting—waiting for another job, another home, for the family he dreamed of having. Waiting to belong. Waiting through years of disappointment had taught him how to expect little. If the donkey didn't respond, that was okay. It would work out eventually.

He felt a sense of irony inside. Did he believe that his own life would work out eventually too? Not really. He had given up on that a long time ago. For the last couple of years, he was just going through the motions. It was too hard to keep dreaming dreams that did not come true.

Until he met Naomi. She had taught him to dream again. She was not afraid to believe. She was not afraid to share her hopes, even if they seemed silly or impossible. He glanced over his shoulder and saw that she had gotten hold of both ropes. She grinned and he smiled back. "We've got this," she whispered.

He hoped that she meant that about more than just the animals.

Peanut took another step forward, brayed, and lowered her head. "That's it," Gideon murmured. "Here you go."

The donkey grabbed the apple slice with her big front teeth, then jerked her head back. She watched him as she chomped the apple. She swallowed and stepped forward for another slice. "It's *gut*, ain't so?"

She ate another slice, then a third. Gideon slowly eased to his feet. "Let's have another slice on the trailer, *ya*?" He held up the slice as he walked backward, toward the ramp. Peanut ambled after him, sniffing and braying. She trotted up the ramp behind him, rattling the metal with her hooves. He gave her the apple as soon as she made it into the trailer. The sheep baaed as they scooted aside to make room. The rabbits watched from their hutch.

"You coming?" Gideon asked Sol.

The camel stared at Peanut and Gideon.

Peanut swallowed the apple and heehawed.

The camel stared for another few beats, then unfolded himself and rose to his feet in a slow, tilting movement. Naomi gasped, then clapped her hand over her mouth to silence herself. Gideon grinned. Sol lumbered to the trailer, then plodded up the ramp, making it shake beneath his weight. As soon as he was aboard, the camel turned to Gideon with a look of aloof disdain, clearly demanding his apple slice. Gideon laughed and handed it over. For the first time in years, he felt like things were going in his favor. Maybe *Gott* would answer his prayers, after all.

Naomi could not be happier. The next few days flew by in a carousel of joyful moments. She and Gideon coaxed the animals into trusting them, slowly but surely. Gideon led the effort in his gentle, quiet way, but refused to take the credit. "You're so sweet, they can't help but love you," he kept telling her.

She noticed how he lingered beside her, drawing out quiet moments together. Sometimes, during those lovely moments as they hand-fed the animals to gain their trust, Gideon would suddenly pull back and make up an excuse to leave. Naomi hoped that he was just worried about getting too close, but doubt kept creeping back in. Especially when he did not say anything about wanting to court her. She had been so worried about him wanting to court her for the wrong reasons that she had not thought to worry about his not wanting to court her at all.

But what if he didn't want their time together to turn into something more? What if he wanted to keep their relationship strictly friendship? What did it actually mean to *like* someone? Her knowledge of love, which was largely confined to the pages of romance novels, did not give any guidance on this. Friends who were perfect for each other were supposed to fall in love, weren't they? It would be preposterous if someone as perfect for her as Gideon did not want to be more than friends. Didn't he feel the tension between them? Didn't he feel the flash of connection when their eyes met?

She had to stop thinking about it because her mind was just going in ridiculous loops, obsessing about the same thing over and over again. First, she worried that he wanted to take advantage of her naivete, then she worried that he didn't want to be with her at all. It was maddening.

The work helped to distract her, especially when the entire family pitched in. John's hammer rang out for several days, until he had constructed a new shelter and pens for the petting zoo. Benjamin helped John out, taking the buggy to the lumberyard for more wood, helping him measure and saw, or hammering alongside him. Emma and Leah brought the babies out to the animals every afternoon before their naps. Caleb and Abby loved to watch the camel lope across the farmyard, the donkey close behind, followed by the pig trotting on her short little legs with her belly almost scraping the ground. They laughed and bounced up and down in their mothers' arms, trying to get closer. Katie rushed home from school every day to make the afternoon feeding. She was determined to win Sol and Peanut over. Amanda and David were busy taking care of the goats most of the time, but Naomi noticed that they lingered by the pens to offer a clandestine orange or handful of grapes whenever they passed by.

Even Miriam smiled when she saw the unlikely mix of animals. Naomi had been worried that she would protest having such unusual animals—especially the camel—but when the hired trailer had arrived to unload them, she just shook her head and rolled her eyes. "Classic Naomi," she had said before heading inside to put supper on. But she could not hide her smile. And later that night, Naomi had caught her trying to pet Sol, while he peered down at her with a haughty look. Even Miriam could not resist his charms.

Sol and Peanut really were the best of friends. Wherever one went, the other followed, even it meant scattering the chickens or trotting through Belinda's plastic baby pool. This outraged the guard goose, sending her on attack mode against the intruders, but Sol just kept loping along, unperturbed. Peanut stopped to plant her hooves wide, thrust out her head, and bray at her. Belinda had never encountered an irritable donkey before and the result was a standoff, in which neither one seemed to quite know what to do.

By the fourth day, the animals came running to Gideon when he appeared in the farmyard. Watching the transformation made Naomi's heart swell. How could the animals be wrong about this man?

Gideon always made sure to feed each of them individually, learning their favorite treats and whispering reassuring words as he filled their buckets. By the end of the week, Peanut was following him around and nudging him with her nose to remind him to hand over a snack. Sol still refused to follow orders, but he allowed Gideon to pet him, which felt like a big victory.

Little Miss Cutie liked to lounge in the mud in the corner of the pen, but popped up anytime Naomi or Gideon appeared. She loved to be scratched behind the ears and Naomi spent all of her spare time giving the pig lots of belly rubs. Pretty soon, she followed Naomi around the farmyard like a faithful hound.

"I think they're ready," Gideon said after a week had passed. "We should put up the sign and start advertising the petting zoo."

Naomi grinned. She felt so happy and carefree, as if nothing else mattered. Or at least it was easier to push away her worries when she was distracted by a big event.

Gideon and Naomi spent twenty minutes painting a sheet of plywood in the tack room where Benjamin and Emma kept the supplies for their soap making business. The rough wood walls and the scent of leather made the space familiar and cozy. Gideon was beginning to feel at home here. He could not imagine leaving anymore. It hit him that there were only a few days left before Katie's parents returned. This had to work. He had no other way to prove his worth to Naomi—or to her family—in such a short amount of time.

Naomi stepped back, set down her paintbrush, and studied the sign. It read in big, bold letters: *STONEYBROOK FARM PETTING ZOO NOW OPEN*. "Do you think it looks *gut* enough?" she asked.

"*Ya*, it's *gut* enough. It's great!"

Naomi gave a decisive nod. "Let's put it up and see what happens."

They didn't have to wait long. By the time they'd hung the sign and made it back up the long, winding driveway from the highway, a white minivan was already pulling in. Naomi hopped off the fence, where she had been sitting and dangling her bare feet, and jogged over to the vehicle. Gideon felt suddenly nervous. What if they didn't like the zoo? What if the animals couldn't handle the attention? What if this whole thing was a failure? What if *he* was a failure? What would Naomi think of him then?

She glanced back at him over her shoulder. "You coming?"

"Uh, *ya*, of course."

He took a deep breath and forced himself to go speak to strangers. And *Englisch* strangers at that. He knew he would be tongue-tied the moment he tried to get his English to sound right. He preferred speaking in Pennsylvania Dutch. No one ever laughed at his accent, like they did when he spoke English.

A woman in her early forties opened the door and stepped out. She pushed her sunglasses down from her forehead and over her eyes. "We saw the sign for the petting zoo and my kids made me stop." She laughed. "Okay, to be honest, I'd like to see the animals too."

"We're so glad you stopped by," Naomi said.

The woman turned back to the minivan and shouted into the open driver-side door, "Come on out, kids!" The passenger doors flew open and three children hopped out, all talking at once. They raced each other to the petting zoo pen, then shouted back to their mother to hurry. She smiled. "Looks like they're happy. Which makes me happy, since they're not playing video games or fighting in the back seat."

Gideon chuckled. He had heard that *Englisch* children spent a lot of time in front of screens, but he never understood why. Probably because most *Englisch* children did not get to live on big, beautiful farms like this one. Not even most Amish children got that. He had been on a lot of farms, but none were as picturesque as this one. No wonder he had fallen in love with the place.

But he had fallen in love with Naomi first. It was a package deal. He could not imagine one without the other. Both of them had become home to him. He grinned as Naomi handed the children plastic cups of animal feed, after the mother handed over crisp five-dollar bills.

Gideon watched them lean over the fence and reach for the animals. He would keep a close eye on things to make sure the animals felt comfortable. But he didn't have to worry. Sol kept his distance, while Little Miss Cutie trotted right over and snorted for attention.

"She loves to be scratched behind the ears," Naomi said.

Before long, the pig was lounging on the ground beside the fence while the children rubbed her belly and scratched her head. She snorted and opened her mouth in what looked suspiciously like a smile.

"Is the petting zoo open now?" Katie's voice carried

across the farmyard. Gideon looked up to see her climbing over the fence to cut the distance between them and the one-room schoolhouse. She dropped her books on the ground and bounded over to the animal pens. "Hi, I'm Katie," she said to the tourists, then thrust her hand into the pen to help them give the pig a good belly rub.

Gideon watched the *Englisch* and Amish *kinner.* They didn't point out their differences or push the other away. They just giggled and chatted and laughed. If they could get along, maybe there was a chance for him to belong here. He was Amish, after all. He was not a stranger, an *Englischer.* He was one of them, even if he did not always feel like it.

Naomi drew closer to him. "They're so cute, aren't they?"

"The *kinner* or the animals?"

Naomi laughed. "Both."

Gideon liked the feeling of Naomi's shoulder against his arm. He liked watching their zoo take off and feeling a part of her family. And, as he felt that warm glow of success, he couldn't help but imagine their own children playing in the farmyard. Did he dare let down his protective walls and admit to Naomi how he really felt—and how much he wanted to stay at Stoneybrook Farm because of her?

Chapter Thirteen

The day flew by. Naomi could not believe how many cars came to the farm to see the petting zoo.

"Our milk sales are up," Leah said as she passed by with glass milk bottles tucked beneath each arm.

"And so are our soap sales," Emma added as she carried a paper bag full of lavender-scented goat milk soap to a red pickup truck. The couple paid in cash, waved to everyone in the farmyard, and reversed. Gravel flew up and the chickens scurried away in a flutter of flapping wings and indignant squawks.

"Come again soon!" Naomi shouted. Her smile was wider than ever. Miriam would see that Gideon's idea was a good one. It could be a big first step to winning her over. Not to mention that she, Naomi, had been a key player in improving sales. And they always said that she was too flighty to be good at business. Ha!

Naomi was feeling rather smug when it was finally time to close up the petting zoo for the evening. The farmyard felt quiet and empty after an afternoon of busy activity. Once the last animal was fed, watered, and tucked away for the night, she exhaled, shook the straw from her apron, and turned to Gideon. "I think we did it."

Gideon inhaled, smiled, and exhaled slowly. "We did."

They watched Little Miss Cutie napping in her mud puddle. Her nose twitched as she snored. Gideon leaned his forearms over the top of the fence and relaxed. He looked so casual, so natural. She had never seen him so at ease before. He was usually quiet and withdrawn. But not now, not when it was just them.

"I hope it goes this well tomorrow too," Naomi said. She wanted to say that she hoped they got to spend every day together like this, but she held back.

"You were *wunderbar*," he said. His blue eyes looked so genuine.

"So were you." The words came out in a whisper. Naomi tore her gaze away from his to glance around. There was no one else nearby. She could hear the soft whirr of the diesel-powered milking machine in the goat shed and the occasional clink of metal. Dishes clanged inside the kitchen and the noise carried through the open window and across the still air. But no one could see them there, in front of the new petting zoo shed, facing the empty driveway.

Naomi felt unexpectedly self-conscious. Her eyes darted to Gideon, then down to her dress. She picked a piece of straw from the bodice, then shook the wrinkles from the skirt.

"It's beautiful, *ya*?" Gideon asked.

Naomi looked up and noticed the sunset spreading across the sky. Golden clouds glowed above the horizon as the blue sky softened into a hazy purple. All around them, the world was settling into a calm silence, like the space between her breath as she held it, waiting to see what might happen between Gideon and her.

"*Ya*." They stood side by side, his arm brushing against hers, in the stillness, neither speaking for a moment.

"I want to tell you something," Gideon said. He pushed away from the fence to face her.

"What is it?" Naomi could see the concern behind his eyes and in the tightness of his jaw.

"It isn't easy to say."

"It's okay. You can trust me."

"I know I can." Gideon smiled and it reached his eyes. So often, when he smiled at other people, it stopped at his mouth and she knew that he was not comfortable. But with her, his eyes always smiled too. Naomi nodded. "Go on."

Gideon chuckled. "I guess I'm nervous. Sometimes I laugh when I'm nervous. Or I just stop talking or, worst of all, I talk too much, because I feel like I have to explain myself. That's what I'm doing right now. Talking too much." He took off his straw hat and raked his fingers through his hair.

"You're talking just the right amount. Say whatever you need to say. I'll be here for as long as it takes."

Some of the tension left Gideon's body. Naomi could see his shoulders lower, just a little, and his jawline did not look as tense anymore. He swallowed. "*Vell*, the truth is, I've been running from my feelings."

"Your feelings?"

"For…you."

"For me?" She held her breath, waiting to hear what she had been waiting a lifetime to hear.

"*Ya*." He turned his hat in his hands. "I've fallen for you. Head over heels. You're…everything. I don't really know how to put it into words."

Naomi could not stop from grinning. "You're doing a *gut* job so far."

"Oh, I am?" He shoved his hat back onto his head. "*Oll recht. Vell, gut.*"

"You don't have to be so nervous."

Gideon raised his eyebrows. "Pretty hard not to be nervous about a thing like this. I don't want to lose you, Naomi." He frowned. "I mean, we're not courting, so I didn't mean to imply…it's just I can't—"

"I know what you mean," Naomi interrupted.

Gideon let out a sharp breath. "Okay. *Gut*."

Naomi wasn't sure this could be real. All her dreams were coming to life. This was the moment the prince declared his love and they lived happily ever after. It was happening. Really, truly happening.

"I've been afraid to tell you how I feel. *Nee*, more than that, I've been afraid to feel what I feel for you." His brow furrowed and he looked away, over the darkening fields bathed in golden light. "I've never belonged anywhere since my parents died. I've never had a place of my own, people of my own. I've been all alone. And if I ever try to get close to someone, I end up losing them."

Naomi studied his expression. She could see the loss in the sharp angles of his profile, silhouetted against the sunset. "Do you feel like you belong here?"

He hesitated, then turned his head to face her. His blue eyes blazed with emotion. "I feel like I belong when I'm with you. You feel like home to me."

The words were so achingly beautiful that Naomi knew she had to kiss him. She wanted to feel that magical moment she had always read about. She waited, breathless, hoping that he would lean down, toward her, and their lips could meet.

But he did not kiss her. She would have to encourage him a little. "I hope this means that you'll stay here, at Stoneybrook Farm, with me."

"Of course I will, if the rest of the family agrees. It's a *wunderbar* farm. It has everything anyone could ever want, but—"

Naomi cut him off by rising up on her tiptoes. She closed her eyes and leaned toward him. A few painful beats ticked by. And then she felt his lips against hers. It was her first kiss, and it was everything she had imagined it would be. Joy washed over her. She could barely finish the kiss, because she wanted to shout how much she loved him, loved this moment, loved life so much she could barely stand it.

"What's going on?" Miriam's voice.

Naomi tore away from Gideon. How long had Miriam been standing there? The kiss had only lasted an instant, but it had felt like an eternity.

Gideon stepped back fast, his expression hard. Naomi had never seen him look like that before. "I love her, Miriam. We're going to court, if she'll have me."

"And you'll have the farm, ain't so?" Miriam shook her head. "I heard what you said."

Naomi's joy plummeted to the ground, like a bird with a broken wing. How could this be happening?

Gideon could not believe it. He had done everything right. He had kept his distance out of respect for Naomi and her family. He had taken a leap of faith, trusting that *Gott* would catch him this time. So he had exposed all his vulnerabilities, gathered all his courage, and told her how he felt, even though he was terrified of losing her.

But somehow, he had still managed to say the wrong thing. He always did. *It's a* wunderbar *farm. It has everything anyone could ever want.* That was what Miriam had heard. He had sounded like he was trying to swindle a naive young woman. What she hadn't heard was the rest. He had planned to say, *but you're what matters, not the farm.* Naomi had cut him off though. And he was not sorry that she had.

He had never been so happy as when she stood up on her tiptoes, signaling that she wanted him to kiss her.

He had not needed any more encouragement than that.

Gideon had been dreaming of kissing Naomi for a very long time. And it had been a perfect kiss. Even if it was cut short. He would face a thousand angry sisters for a moment like that. No one would keep him from the woman he loved. Not anymore. Not Miriam, and not his own fears.

"You don't have anything to say?" Miriam crossed her arms and glared up at him.

"I've said everything I need to say. To Naomi. It's her life and I think she should decide it."

Miriam raised her eyebrows. "You just admitted that you want the farm. What more proof does she need that you're taking advantage of her—of all of us?"

"Miriam!" Naomi stepped between them. "It wasn't like that. You didn't hear everything."

"I heard enough."

Gideon took a deep breath and then exhaled. He needed to think before he spoke. Tensions were too high.

"I came out here to tell you supper is on the table," Miriam said before Gideon formed a response. "But I'm calling a family meeting. Supper can wait."

Naomi looked from Gideon to Miriam, then back to him. She shook her head. He could see the pain and frustration in her eyes and felt a stab of regret. He had been right to tell her—and Miriam—how he felt. But he didn't want to come between Naomi and her family. None of this was going the way he had planned.

Miriam marched across the yard, ahead of them, to round up the rest of the family. "I'm so sorry, Naomi," Gideon said as soon as Miriam was out of earshot.

"You didn't do anything wrong."

Gideon took a deep breath and reached for her hand. His jaw tensed as he waited for her reaction. She gripped his hand tightly and did not let it go. Her face tilted up to his to look into his eyes. "I'm with you."

"And I'm with you." But Gideon wasn't sure that staying by her side was going to be the best way to solve the problem. How could he prove to her family that he had honorable intentions if he and Naomi insisted that he move into the farmhouse and become one of them? They might give in to Naomi, since she had a say in how things were run, but they would never trust him. They would always look at him with uneasy glances, whisper behind his back, assume the worst. That was not the life he wanted. He wanted to belong. He could not put himself in a situation where no one believed in him. He had been through that for too long.

But he could not leave Naomi. He had to show her how much he loved her. He could not run away when he had finally found a place that felt like home.

A slow realization began to creep down his spine. What if staying wasn't the way to make this relationship work? What if staying wasn't the way to love Naomi?

"What is it?"

Gideon had not realized that he had stopped walking. He looked toward the windows of the farmhouse, where he could see dark shapes moving, but could not make out any details. "I just realized something."

"Something bad?"

Gideon let out a long breath through his clenched teeth. "*Nee.*" He frowned. "*Vell*, it won't feel *gut*. But it would be for the best."

Naomi turned to face him. "Tell me what you're thinking."

"You know how much I want to stay."

Her expression shifted. "Don't say what I think you're about to say."

Gideon squeezed her hand tighter. "What if it's best that I leave? Just for a little while."

Naomi shut her eyes and shook her head. "I told you not to say it. I don't want to hear that." She opened her eyes and stared up at him with big dark eyes, glazed over with moisture.

"I know. I don't want to think about it either. But I think we have to."

A raised voice drifted out of the open window. "He did what?"

"Oh, no," another voice responded.

"Poor Naomi. She's so sweet."

"Too sweet for her own *gut*." Naomi recognized that one as Miriam's voice.

"I'll leave with you," Naomi said. "They think I'm hopeless. They don't understand the first thing about me."

Gideon raised their hands and kissed hers. "I want to take you with me. More than anything. But I can't do that to you. This is your home. And as much as they're hurting your feelings right now, I know they love you. And I know you love them. I'm not going to come between you."

"You wouldn't be coming between us if you stay," Naomi said. "We'll show them that our love is real."

"And how would that make you feel in the meantime—when everyone in the household is on edge?"

Naomi's brow furrowed and she looked down. "I... There has to be a way."

"I think there is," he said in a steady, even voice. Now that he knew what to do, he had never felt so calm or confident. "I have to leave and show them that I'm not with you for the farm and that I'm not pushing a quick courtship. We'll give it time. I won't let you go."

"I don't want to wait."

Gideon paused. Her hand felt warm and right in his. He didn't want to wait either.

Naomi wiped her eye with her free hand. "But I know you're right. If you go, then they'll see you're willing to walk away." Her eyes swung up to his. "But you're not walking away, are you?"

"Nee."

"You'll stay close by, ain't so?"

Gideon exhaled. He did not want to have to tell her his entire plan—to go wherever he needed to, no matter how far or how challenging. He wasn't even sure if it was a good plan. It had just come to him during their conversation, but it felt right. "I'll have to go somewhere where I can make the best living. It might be far away. If I can earn enough, then I can prove that I'm not trying to court you for your money."

"We don't have to prove that to them. It's my life, remember?"

"And I meant it when I told Miriam that. But I also meant it when I said I wouldn't come between you and your family. I've never seen such a tight-knit one before. Even the in-laws. You can't tell who's blood and who's not. It doesn't matter here."

"We like to say that there's always room for one more." Naomi shook her head.

"And there will be, in time," Gideon said. "I just have to prove myself first. I'm willing to do that. I want to be one of you. Not someone who they grudgingly accept because they have to."

"You shouldn't have to prove yourself by making money. That isn't the Amish way."

"Maybe not. But I want to. I need to." His eyes flashed as he realized the enormity of that need. "People have looked down on me for years. I've never amounted to much. I have to show your family that I'm worth something or I'll never be able to feel at home here. Not completely."

"I thought you already felt at home."

Gideon sighed. "I do—more than I ever have anywhere since my parents died. But this would always be hanging over me if I force my way into the family. I'll know they don't really respect me or believe in me. I want to show them who I really am."

"They should see it now. The way I do."

"There's a lot of things that should be, but life doesn't always go as it should."

Naomi leaned closer to him. Darkness had fallen across the farmyard and stars appeared overhead, twinkling in the vast emptiness of space. Gideon watched her watching them. "Okay," she said. "I understand. I want what's best for you."

She was willing to sacrifice being with him if that was what he needed. And he knew that he did. His leaving was as much for him as for her. He realized that now. It was the only way. "I'll write you," he said. "Every day."

Her chin was tilted up as she surveyed the stars. He studied the lines of her face, trying to memorize them before they disappeared. It was hard to follow the rule against photographs sometimes. He noticed the soft curve of her throat, the lively glint in her eyes, the small, upturned nose. He would not forget. Just as he had not forgotten the color of her eyes and eyelashes, though he could not make that out in the darkness. She dropped her gaze to look at him. "I'll write you too. Every day."

He nodded, took her in his arms, and kissed her. And he did not care who might be watching. He would say goodbye the right way. Because he did not know how long it would be before he saw her again.

Chapter Fourteen

Nothing was the same without Gideon. A day passed, then two, as Naomi waited for the first letter. Even the animals seemed sad without him. They kept looking into the distance while they bellowed and stamped their hooves, as if they expected him to appear, and could not understand why he did not. Little Miss Cutie did not trot over for belly rubs. Sol and Peanut wandered their pen in restless circles.

"I know," Naomi said as she passed out apple slices. "I miss him too."

Peanut brayed, then lunged for an apple slice. But Sol hung back, looking down through narrowed eyes. He snorted then loped away, tail swishing, and big feet throwing up dust.

Naomi sighed. She had fallen in love with the animals, but she felt in over her head without Gideon. His presence had been so calming and reassuring. Even when he didn't speak, he had made her feel safe, just standing near in his quiet, thoughtful way.

And, now, she did not know when he would stand beside her again. Her sisters had been surprised when he announced that he was leaving. He had not stayed long enough to discuss it, but did say that he wanted to make his own way in life, before courting Naomi.

"I'll be back for her," he had said before striding away with his green duffel bag slung over his shoulder.

But now, Naomi wasn't so sure. People liked to say that absence makes the heart grow fonder. And it was a very romantic notion. But she didn't feel so romantic anymore.

After feeding the animals, she wandered into the farmhouse, even though it was the middle of the afternoon. She needed to escape into her room for a little while and hide. Every time her sisters looked at her, they had that same pitying look in their eyes. She just could not take that anymore. She wanted them to see that she and Gideon knew what they were doing. She wanted to prove that she was capable of seeing good from bad, and that she wasn't silly or flighty.

But as the hours ticked by, the doubt weighed heavier and heavier within her. What if he was just looking for an easy excuse to leave? He might have realized that getting his hands on the farm wasn't worth the effort. It would be easier for him to start over somewhere new, without complications from suspicious in-laws. Or potential in-laws. He had never made a promise to marry her. They had not even agreed to court.

But he had said he would come back. That should be enough.

But it wasn't.

Naomi slipped into her room, shut the door, and sank onto her bed. The mattress creaked under her weight. She stared at the wooden hope chest across the room. All of her treasures were inside. A double wedding ring quilt she had lovingly stitched to use after she was married. The recipe card that Naomi had memorized years ago, but kept because it was in her mother's handwriting. A set of handsewn white linen table napkins. And her stash of romance novels. Usually, at a time like this, when she was feeling heartsick, Naomi would pull one out and steal a few minutes to devour a chapter or two. Afterward, she would always feel refreshed and inspired.

But not today. Love did not seem so real anymore. Romance had lost its luster. This was the real world, not a fantasy on a page. Maybe Miriam was right and it was time to get her head out of the clouds. She could not hold on to her dreams forever. She should be practical. Otherwise, she would not be able to bear the disappointment if Gideon let her down.

Naomi felt something slipping away inside her. It was the deep, unyielding belief that love would conquer all. Maybe she was finally growing up. If so, she wasn't sure she liked the new her.

There was a knock at the door and Naomi straightened up. "*Kumme* in."

The door swung open and Benjamin bounded inside. "Your first letter came."

"You mean…?"

Benjamin grinned and held out the letter, just out of reach.

Naomi's heart flip-flopped in her chest. "Give it to me!"

Benjamin laughed. "Say please."

She leaped up to grab it, but he held the letter just out of reach, above her head.

"Please," she half yelled, half laughed as she jumped up and down, trying to reach it.

He let her grab it from him and he grinned as she tore it open.

"I knew he'd write!"

Benjamin raised his eyebrows. "Then why have you been moping around for the past two days?"

"Shh, I'm reading." Naomi scanned the letter, taking in every word as quickly as she could. Gideon was staying at

Viola's but only temporarily. He would be leaving for Maine tomorrow, where one of Edna Yoder's cousins had a blueberry farm in need of a good worker. It wouldn't be enough money to prove anything yet, but it was a start.

Benjamin's expression fell as he watched her read. "It's not *gut* news?"

"It is, it's just…" She dropped the letter onto the bed and tried to dab at a tear with her sleeve without Benjamin noticing. How long would she and Gideon be apart now? And did he really mean what he had written?

"If he really does love you, then he'll prove it to you," Benjamin said.

"We're not courting. Not officially."

"That doesn't mean he doesn't love you."

"Maybe love doesn't matter in a situation like this. Sometimes things just don't work out."

Benjamin flinched. "Naomi, what's gotten into you? You sound like a stranger."

Naomi snorted. "*Nee*, I sound like Miriam."

Benjamin rubbed the back of his neck. "You know that Miriam—all of us—we just want what's best for you. I've been worried, same as the rest of the family."

"*Ya*, but can't you see that I need to be the one to decide my future?"

"I know what it's like for people not to believe you can handle your own life. Remember how hard Miriam fought against Emma and me getting together?"

"*Ach*, I remember, all right."

"Then you also remember that you were fighting us along with Miriam."

Naomi frowned. "Not as much as Amanda was."

"It was enough."

"I was just worried."

"Exactly."

"*Oll recht*. Fine." Naomi sighed. "I get your point. But I'm still upset."

"That's okay."

"It doesn't feel okay."

"You know, I never thought things could work out between Emma and me, but here we are, and she's one of us now."

"She's never been arrested. She wasn't a drifter who nobody trusts."

"She went through plenty though. Having a baby out of wedlock isn't easy in our community."

Naomi didn't answer. She breathed in and exhaled slowly. "So, what are you trying to say?"

Benjamin shrugged and flashed his signature grin. "I don't know. Just that you're not as alone as you feel. I'm rooting for you and Gideon, if he really is genuine. And all of us want you to end up happy."

"Happy and alone."

"*Nee*, happy with the right man."

"How is he going to be able to prove to everyone that he's the right one?"

Benjamin tucked his thumbs into his suspenders and thought for a moment. "I don't know. But I don't think making money is the way to do it."

"But Miriam is convinced that he's after the farm because he doesn't have any money."

"*Ya*, but…"

"What?"

Benjamin furrowed his brow. "I don't know. It feels worldly to me. Like something the *Englisch* would do. I think there's a better way for him to show us that he's got a *gut* heart."

"*Vell,* how?"

"Oh, I have no idea. That's for you to figure out."

The sound of a baby's cries drifted through the walls. "Sounds like Caleb's up from his nap," Benjamin said. "Gotta go."

Naomi was left wondering how to show who Gideon really was. She realized that no matter how much he earned, it wouldn't prove anything to her. And, if something didn't stop him from going to Maine, he would be gone for weeks or months.

And then what?

Gideon had a deep, unsettling worry that he was doing the wrong thing. But he also felt a drive to prove himself that he could not deny. Wasn't he doing the right thing to show everyone—including Naomi—that he could earn a good living and support her on his own? Wasn't that what being a man was all about?

The sound of Viola's cane thudded down the hallway and into the living room, where Gideon was stacking firewood. He set the last log onto the hearth, straightened up, and stretched his back.

"You're really going to leave tomorrow?" Viola stared at him above her glasses, which sat low on her nose.

"*Ya.* I don't have a choice."

"Pffft. You could find a job here."

"I've already got a good offer in Maine. I shouldn't let it go. That would be irresponsible. And, I've already told you, the whole point is to prove I'm dependable." Gideon hoped he had not sounded too sharp, but her questions were making him feel even more uncomfortable with his decision.

"You've told me, but that doesn't mean I agree."

Gideon smiled. "Fair enough."

"And what about those animals at the petting zoo I've heard about?"

"You heard about that?" Gideon felt a swell of pride. Maybe he wasn't such a failure after all. Word was getting around. "What, uh, exactly did you hear?"

"That you did a *lecherich* thing, buying animals that nobody wanted and that won't be easy to take care of."

Gideon deflated. "Oh. They think it's ridiculous?"

"Some folks do." Viola shrugged. "But that doesn't matter. I think it's a *wunderbar* idea, and so do the tourists, ain't so? I hear it was real busy on opening day."

Gideon tilted his head. "How did you know—"

Viola waved her hand. "Edna mentioned all the traffic coming up and down the driveway. She could see it from her kitchen window."

Gideon smiled at the memory. "*Ya.* It was a *gut* day." He remembered how happy Naomi had been and how she had believed in his idea.

Viola hobbled to her armchair, braced her hands on her cane, and lowered herself onto the seat. She sighed and propped her feet up on the ottoman. "Now, what are you thinking, leaving Naomi to take care of those animals by herself?"

Gideon frowned. "It isn't like that."

"Then *kumme* tell me what it's like."

"I've got another log to split before I go tomorrow. I want to leave you with plenty of firewood."

"That can wait." Viola lifted her cane and pointed to the sofa. "Sit."

Gideon shook his head. Viola was not going to take no for an answer.

"Oh, and why don't you grab the cookie tin from the kitchen counter on your way to the sofa?"

Gideon smiled. The kitchen was definitely not on the way to the sofa, but Viola wouldn't let something like that stop her. He thought about how to explain himself to Viola while he walked across the hall to the kitchen, grabbed the tin, and doubled back to the living room.

"Plates?"

"Uh, sorry, I forgot." He turned around to head back to the kitchen.

"We don't need them. It's just us. *Kumme* sit. And have a cookie. Oatmeal raisin."

Gideon sank down onto the sofa. Viola popped open the tin and he grabbed a cookie, but didn't take a bite. His stomach was too on edge.

"So, you were telling me why you've abandoned Naomi and the animals in your petting zoo."

"*Vell*, I wouldn't put it quite that way."

Viola raised an eyebrow.

He didn't know what else to say, so he said nothing.

Viola swallowed and wiped her mouth with her sleeve. "Then how would you put it?"

Gideon looked down. He turned the cookie slowly in his hands. "It's for the best. Miriam—the whole family really—they'll never accept me until I show them I'm worth something."

"And Naomi?"

"I need to show her too."

"Need to or *want* to?"

He frowned. "Isn't it the same thing?"

Viola grunted. "Not at all."

"Okay, then I think it's both."

"So you're going to go off to Maine, earn a lot of money, and come back one day with enough cash to show them all that you'll make a *gut* husband?"

"Something like that."

"Are you Amish or *Englisch*? We don't put stock in worldly treasures."

"We still have to eat. And live. I have to provide for Naomi."

"She's already provided for. Stoneybrook Farm makes all the money either of you will need."

Gideon shifted in his seat. "I have to contribute something."

Viola leaned forward and pointed a bony finger at him. "You think all a man has to contribute is a living? You think if you bring in the money for your family, then you'll be somebody?"

"*Vell, ya.*" Gideon slumped back against the back of the couch and sighed. "It's not that complicated."

Viola cackled. Then she bit into her cookie and chewed as she shook her head.

"Why are you laughing?"

Viola shook her head again, then swallowed. She patted her mouth. "If you don't know, I can't tell you. I'm going to be praying that you find out. And fast—before it's too late."

Gideon had been looked down on long enough to know that things like this mattered. He was pretty sure that he understood what Viola was getting at, but it was one thing to say something, and another to have to live it. And he'd lived being the one who no one thought was good enough.

He wanted to march back to Stoneybrook Farm, storm into the house, and tell them all that he was more than a nobody. That he was a *somebody.* And that he mattered. But he felt too ashamed to even think about it. Because he knew that no one would see it.

Except Naomi. Maybe. But even if she did, didn't he owe

her more than what he had been giving her? She deserved better. And he would find a way to give more to her.

He just hoped that he didn't lose himself in the process.

Naomi could not get Peanut to settle down. She had been restless all day, braying and kicking her back legs, until Naomi fed her extra apples and sat down with her in the pen. "You miss Gideon, ain't so? He was the only one who could keep you calm."

Peanut's agitation was contagious, and soon Sol was pacing the farmyard, bellowing and swinging his head in sharp, anxious movements. By suppertime, Naomi felt like giving up. She didn't know what to do. All she wanted was Gideon back at Stoneybrook Farm, where he belonged.

Yes. He belonged here. She believed it deep down. And she also believed that he had made a mistake by leaving. He should prove himself in a better, more meaningful way. He did not need to earn enough to get them started in life. They already had Stoneybrook Farm to run together. But how could she show him that he was needed and wanted for who he was—not for how much he earned? How could she convince Gideon to come back?

And then, of course, there was her family. Sure, Naomi could stand up and insist, and they would probably, eventually, go along with it. But at what cost? Would Gideon ever really feel at home if her sisters only welcomed him because they felt they had to?

Naomi closed the gate to the petting zoo pen and sighed. Peanut trotted over and swung her head over the fence. Sol lay on the ground nearby, watching them through lazy, half-closed lids as he chewed his cud in a sideways motion. Peanut snorted when Naomi scratched behind her ears and pushed her muzzle into her shoulder. "Easy, now." Naomi laughed.

"You'll push me over if you're not careful. You're stronger than you look."

Peanut heehawed and stared at her with her wet, black eyes.

"*Ach*, you want another apple slice." She held up her hands. "All gone. You can have more tomorrow."

Peanut gave another loud heehaw that carried across the farmyard and made the chickens cluck and ruffle their feathers. Belinda marched around the corner of the petting zoo shed to investigate.

"If I didn't know any better, I'd think you could understand me," Naomi said to Peanut. "But you just won't take *nee* for an answer."

"You know, I don't want to admit it, but Peanut's growing on me," Miriam said from a distance away.

Naomi turned to see Miriam striding across the farmyard. "No one can resist loving Peanut," Naomi said. "Even you."

"Even me." Miriam smiled but her eyes did not.

Naomi stiffened. She could sense a lecture coming on by the subtle strain on Miriam's face. "What is it?"

"I came to tell you dinner is on the table."

Naomi stepped away from the fence. Peanut thrust her head forward and brayed.

"I'll be back soon," Naomi said to Peanut, then began walking toward Miriam. "That's all you wanted to say?"

Miriam frowned and adjusted her *kapp*. "I just want to make sure you're *oll recht*."

"Of course I'm not all right. Gideon's gone and I don't know when he's coming back."

They walked a few steps in silence. "And you blame me for that," Miriam said after a moment.

"*Vell*... *Ya*. I guess I do."

"That's fair. I'm the one who's been the most concerned about him."

"And by most concerned, you mean that you think he's a criminal."

"I never said that."

Naomi snorted. "You may as well have."

Miriam exhaled and stopped walking. "Look, I know it's hard. I know *I* can be hard."

"For certain sure."

Miriam put up her hand. "I'm trying to—"

"Apologize?"

"*Ach, vell* maybe not that exactly…"

Naomi raised her eyebrows.

"Explain. I'm trying to explain."

Naomi shook her head. "Is that what you're calling it now?"

"*Oll recht*. Fine. You're right. I owe you an apology for being a little too harsh. I didn't mean to drive Gideon away or to hurt you, and I'm sorry for that."

"A *little* too harsh?"

"I welcomed him in. I didn't turn him away."

"You didn't welcome him in, in here." Naomi pointed to Miriam's chest, right over her heart.

"You know I have to protect you. It's my job. And I can't be sorry for that."

"Can you be sorry for how you've made him feel? I'm not the only one you've hurt."

Miriam closed her eyes and pinched the bridge of her nose. "*Ya*. Of course." She dropped her hand and opened her eyes. "I don't want to hurt anyone. You have to know that."

Naomi crossed her arms and looked away. "*Ya*. I know that. But you still did, whether you meant to or not."

"I have to be sure he's *gut* for you. Can't you see that?"

"Can't you see that it's time to let go and let me decide that?"

"Sometimes you need an outside opinion when it comes to matters of the heart. And I don't just mean you personally. I mean anyone. Love can blind people."

"So you think it's love." Naomi narrowed her eyes.

"I didn't say that." Miriam shook her head. "Look, you're having strong emotions—"

"So do you think it's love or not?"

Miriam threw up her hands. "I don't know."

"That means you think it might be." Naomi felt a ripple of hope. Miriam was softening. Maybe she was beginning to see who Gideon really was.

Miriam inhaled and let out a long, deep breath. "It could be. But that's the problem. We can't know. He needs to show us. Actions, not words."

Naomi grabbed Miriam's arm. "He's doing that. It's why he left. To show that he can support me, that he isn't just looking for a handout. He wants you to see that he's worth something."

"*Ya*. I know." Miriam put her hand over Naomi's. "I see what he's trying to do."

"You do?"

"Of course I do. He's taking the harder path…unless…" Miriam gave Naomi a sidelong glance.

"Unless what?"

"What if he's leaving because he's not willing to do the hard work and commit to you?"

Indignation seared through Naomi. Or was it fear? This was her unspoken worry. She had buried it so deep that she would not say it out loud. "Of course he's committed. He left so that we can be together."

"When?"

"Eventually!"

Miriam squeezed Naomi's hand and let it go. "I hope you're right."

Naomi glared at Miriam. "Do you really?"

Miriam's expression cracked. "Of course I do. I want you to be happy. And if that's what makes you happy—if he's as genuine as you say he is, then yes, that is one hundred percent what I want." Miriam's face regained its usual calm. "Surely you can see that."

Naomi frowned. She didn't know what to say.

Miriam's gaze moved over the farmyard, to the view beyond the barn where the land sloped downward into the Yoders' sunflower field. "One day you'll see. Even if you can't now."

"I'm not a child, Miriam."

"That doesn't mean that you see that I've discouraged Gideon from courting you because I love you."

Naomi exhaled through her teeth. "I see it. But I just think you're wrong."

Miriam nodded. Belinda honked from behind the chicken coop and one of the hens flapped her wings. Ollie the guard dog barked somewhere in the distance. "Let's go inside," Miriam said.

Naomi knew there was nothing else to say. Miriam was softening, but she still had far to go. And every moment Gideon stayed away was a moment that Naomi felt a little piece of her heart breaking apart.

Chapter Fifteen

Naomi and Miriam left the front door open when they came inside for dinner. The day was hot and the farmhouse needed the breeze. Cool air swept in through the screen door and dining room windows, carrying the scent of fresh-cut grass and sunshine. During the meal, Naomi missed turning to the side and shooting Gideon a knowing look. He was the only person she knew who could communicate so well without a single word.

The rest of the family chatted and fought over the last biscuit, then devoured three apple pies. It almost seemed like nobody noticed that Gideon was gone, but Naomi picked up on the awkward glances and careful conversation. No one wanted to address the situation. But it was clear her sisters felt guilty. Miriam kept a frown on her face as she went through the motions of clearing her plate. Amanda picked at the honey-baked ham without eating it. Leah whispered at John, they both shook their heads, then looked down.

Benjamin drained his glass of goat milk in a succession of gulps, then set down the glass with a bang and wiped his mouth with his sleeve. "You okay, Naomi?" he asked.

Naomi almost said she was fine. But she did not. Maybe it was finally time to tell the truth and force the family to confront the situation. Naomi set down her fork. The clang startled Abby, who was sitting in John's lap as he fed her mashed sweet potatoes, and she stopped eating and stared at Naomi with big, blue eyes.

"*Nee*," Naomi said softly. "I'm not okay."

The room fell into sudden silence as everyone's attention swung her way. She opened her mouth to speak when she was interrupted by a loud heehaw, followed by a crash, a bang, and then the clip-clop of hooves traipsing across hardwood floor.

Miriam shot up from her chair.

Leah's eyes widened.

John stumbled up so fast that that his chair knocked over backward.

Amanda laughed and Miriam shot her a look.

"Peanut?" Naomi stood up fast. Everyone was going to blame her for this. And, worst of all, she knew that the donkey would not listen to her. Peanut only listened to one person—and he was not here.

There was another loud heehaw, followed by the quick clatter of hooves, a thud against a wall, more clatter, then Peanut's head appeared around the corner of the dining room door.

"Get her out of here!" Miriam shouted.

Caleb squealed in delight. Abby squirmed in John's lap and reached toward the doorway.

"Come on, Peanut, let's get you back outside," Naomi said. She tried to keep her voice calm, but authoritative. She must not have struck the right balance because Peanut just stared at her from the doorway.

Miriam grabbed a cloth napkin and waved it toward the donkey. "Shoo! Go on now! Get out of here!"

"How did she get in here?" Leah asked.

"Through the screen door," Benjamin said.

"*Vell*, I know that, but how did it happen? Wasn't the petting zoo gate latched?"

Naomi thought back to when she had closed the gate. She had latched it, hadn't she? Naomi frowned. She had been distracted, her thoughts on Gideon.

"You were the last one out of the pen," Amanda said to Naomi.

"It's *oll recht*," Naomi said. "I'll fix it." She stepped toward Peanut, but the donkey turned around fast and trotted away, head held high.

"She knows exactly what she's doing," Amanda said.

"You're not making this any better," Miriam muttered.

Amanda laughed, then the babies began laughing.

"She's probably leaving," Naomi said. "But I'll make sure."

But the sound of hoofbeats was moving in the opposite direction from the front door. Naomi dashed after Peanut and chased her into the kitchen. Peanut brayed and stamped a hoof, then circled the room. Footsteps pounded down the hall, followed by one family member after another piling into the threshold, watching the scene unfold. "Not the kitchen!" Miriam wailed. Amanda laughed even harder than before. Caleb bounced in Benjamin's arms and Abby gurgled and cooed as she tried to wiggle out of John's arms to get closer.

Peanut trotted toward the counter and Miriam dashed across the room to head her off. Naomi ran around the other side and blocked her path. But Peanut made a sharp turn and crashed into the kitchen table. The wood shuddered and the legs scraped against the floor. A pitcher of lemonade toppled over and liquid poured across the table, onto the floor, and splattered across Naomi's feet. "Peanut!" she shouted.

The donkey reached down, plunged her muzzle into the fruit basket, and bit into a shiny red apple. She raised her head and crunched into it with a satisfied glint in her eye.

"She just wanted an apple," Naomi said.

"*Vell*, get her out of here before she does some real damage," Miriam said.

Naomi stepped to Peanut's side and gave her a soft pat on the rump. "Come on now. You've got your apple. Let's get you back to the barn." But the donkey did not budge. She planted her hooves into the floor and lowered her head. Naomi gave her a gentle push. The donkey stood as solid as a wall, crunching the apple.

"She's not going to listen to you, is she?" Benjamin asked.

"Um..." Naomi swallowed hard. "*Nee*."

There was a crash across the house, followed by a soft scraping sound, a loud thump, and heavy footfalls against wood.

"What in the world..." Miriam hitched up her skirt and sprinted out of the kitchen. After a few beats, they heard her shout, "You cannot be serious!" A moment later, Sol's big eyes peered around the doorway. He hesitated, staring at them through his long lashes, then saw Peanut, and loped into the kitchen.

Leah gasped.

David jumped aside to make room before he was knocked down.

John passed Abby over to Leah, then waved his arms to head the camel off, but Sol just ambled past him.

Miriam grabbed the broom and shook it at Sol.

Amanda just kept laughing.

Sol didn't acknowledge any of them. Instead, he lumbered over to Peanut, folded his long legs beneath him, and kneeled down onto the floor with a satisfied sigh. His eyelids half closed and he began to slowly chew his cud.

"He's not getting up," Miriam said, still stabbing at the air with the broom. "You've got to do something, Naomi. This is *your* petting zoo. These animals are supposed to listen to you."

"But they don't," Amanda said. "They only listen to Gideon."

"It's his zoo," Naomi said. "It was his idea and they're his animals. He's got a way with them. No one else can make them feel safe like he does."

"We don't need to make them feel safe," Miriam said. "We just need to make them move."

"They have to feel safe before they'll do what we want."

Miriam set down the broom. "Nice donkey," she said in the high-pitched tone of voice reserved for babies and cute kittens. "Nice camel."

Amanda rolled her eyes. "Miriam, you are not going to convince them that way."

Benjamin laughed. "It's not working at all."

Miriam threw up her hands. "Fine. You try."

They all did. John tried to push them out, since he was the biggest. Benjamin and David joined in, but none of them could make the animals move. Sol just flicked his tail and glared at them. Peanut widened her stance, braced her legs, dropped her apple, thrust her head forward, and heehawed so loudly it made Naomi's ears ring. The men gave up and stepped back. Benjamin rubbed the back of his neck. "I don't think we're going to get them out."

"And they're in the kitchen of all places!" Miriam said as she glared at the animals with her hands on her hips.

Naomi realized that this was the moment she had been waiting for. Hope sparked inside her and she clasped her hands together. Could it be that *Gott* had answered her prayers in the most unexpected way?

"Naomi's got an idea," Leah said. "I can see it on her face."

Everyone's attention swung to her.

Naomi realized that she was smiling. She tried to force a more authoritative expression so they would take her more seriously. "*Ya*. I do. And it's the only thing that will work."

Everyone stared at her, even Sol, who continued to chew his cud as he lounged on the floor beside Peanut. "We have to get Gideon."

The room erupted into low murmurs and everyone talked at once.

Miriam held up a hand. "She's right."

The room fell silent.

Naomi's eyes narrowed. "You agree with me?"

Miriam smiled and shook her head. "*Ya*. Believe it or not, I do. I've seen him with the animals. And I need to get these two out of my kitchen—now."

Naomi's face erupted in a grin.

She didn't waste a second. She was already running out the door before remembering to yell back, "I'll get him and we'll be back right away!"

Gideon was rolling his spare shirt to fit it into his army-green duffel bag when a shout caught his attention. He dropped the shirt and dashed out of Viola's spare bedroom, through her living room, and threw open the front door. The sound of Viola's cane was close behind, tapping against the linoleum floor as she hurried to catch up.

Naomi was running up the front porch steps, eyes flashing with what looked like excitement. Or fear.

"What's wrong?"

Naomi shook her head as she caught her breath. "Nothing. Not really. I mean—just *kumme* with me. I'll explain everything on the way."

"Is it an emergency?" Gideon grabbed his straw hat from the hook by the door.

"*Nee*, it's an answer to prayer." Naomi grabbed Gideon's hand, pulling him along as she hurried toward the buggy.

Gideon glanced back to Viola as he jogged behind Naomi.

"Go on," she said and waved her cane at him. "Then be sure to tell me all about it."

"So you can tell everyone in Bluebird Hills," Naomi shouted back.

Viola cackled as she watched them stumble into the buggy. "For certain sure."

Naomi filled Gideon in on the details as the buggy rumbled down the back roads, whisking them toward Stoneybrook Farm. He tapped his foot at every stop sign. He needed to get there as fast as he could.

"Don't you see?" Naomi asked. "You're the only one who can get Peanut and Sol to listen."

"*Ya*, but what if they don't listen this time?"

"They will." Naomi flicked the reins. "I know they will."

Gideon exhaled. "I don't want to disappoint you."

"You could never disappoint me."

Gideon knew that wasn't true. There were plenty of things he could do to let her down.

"All you have to do is be yourself. Like always."

Gideon scratched his head. He wasn't too worried about getting Peanut and Sol to follow him out of the house. But it seemed like Naomi had a lot more riding on this. He could sense that she wanted him to prove himself to everyone. And he wasn't sure that was going to work. He looked over at her. She glanced at him, grinned, and flicked the reins again. "You've got this."

He started to tell her that she shouldn't count on her family changing their mind about him. But instead, he swallowed hard, stared straight ahead at the golden wheat waving in the fields, and whispered a prayer to *Gott*.

When they pulled into the farmyard, the sound of Peanut's high-pitched braying drifted across the warm, still air. "Poor little fellow," Gideon said as he hopped down from the buggy.

"More like poor Miriam. Peanut is having a great time."

They both laughed as they jogged across the muddy farmyard, skirted the chicken coop, and sidestepped a brown hen.

When they reached the front door, Gideon saw the ripped screen where Peanut, then Sol, had torn their way through. "A full-grown camel never could have fit," Gideon said. "But it must have still been a tight squeeze for Sol."

"Can you imagine what he'll do when he is full-grown?" Naomi asked as they opened the battered screen door. It creaked, shuddered, and fell from its hinges. Gideon caught the wooden frame before it could hit Naomi.

"Nice save," she said as she ducked out of the way.

Gideon shook his head. "Those two really wanted to get in."

"They were probably looking for you." Naomi glanced back at him as they hurried down the hall. "And apples too. But I think you're what they really wanted."

No one had ever been that loyal to him before. Sure, Sol and Peanut were animals, not people, but it still meant something to him. He felt a surge of confidence as he rounded the corner into the kitchen. The scene looked like something out of a children's book. Two farm animals had taken over the kitchen, people were pushing and pulling at them, everyone was talking at once, and the camel and the donkey seemed blissfully unconcerned as they rummaged through whatever they could find, sniffing and snorting at all the mysterious foods and smells.

A basket of fruit lay overturned on the kitchen table, the apples, lemons, and pears strewn across the floor; a pitcher had rolled onto the floor surrounded by a puddle of lemonade; and a sack of flour lay open on the counter, its contents spilled everywhere. White, powdery footprints in the shape of hooves crisscrossed the kitchen floor and Peanut's muzzle was dusted with flour. Gideon could not help but grin. Until he saw Miriam's face.

Gideon snapped into a serious expression. "I'll, uh, see what I can do," he said.

Miriam nodded, but kept her frown.

A pulse of anxiety pumped through Gideon's veins. He may have gotten in over his head. And if he couldn't get the animals to listen, then the entire family would think he was unable to live up to expectations. Worst of all, he would disappoint Naomi. Well, he was planning on catching the evening bus to Maine, so at least he would be leaving the humiliation behind him.

Of course, that meant leaving Naomi behind too. The thought sent a stab of alarm through his chest. He tried to ignore it and focus on the problem at hand. "Looks like you've gotten into a little trouble," Gideon said to Peanut. Peanut's head snapped up from where she had been rummaging through a crate of potatoes. The donkey heehawed and trotted over to Gideon with her head held high. Peanut pushed her muzzle against Gideon's shoulder and nuzzled close. Gideon smiled and rubbed the donkey's head. "That's a *gut maedel*," he murmured. "I've missed you. You missed me too, *ya*?"

Sol unfolded his long legs and pushed himself up from the ground rump first in a slow, swaying motion. He loped over to Gideon and rested his long, thick neck over Gideon's shoulder. Gideon chuckled. "Easy now. You don't know your own strength." Sol grunted and pressed closer. Gideon patted Sol on the neck. "*Gut* to see you too, *bu*. Ready to go back outside, where you belong?" Sol grunted again. Peanut pushed against Sol, trying to get closer to Gideon.

"They're so happy to see you," Naomi said.

"I've never seen anything like it before," Leah said.

"We heard what you said from the hallway," John said.

"And I think you're right, Naomi. Those animals came in here looking for Gideon."

Naomi smiled. "For certain sure. They haven't been the same since he left."

Gideon patted Sol on the neck again. "*Oll recht, bu*, let's go. *Kumme*." Gideon whispered a prayer that he really could get Sol and Peanut to follow him. Then he took a deep breath, turned around, and headed out the door. He held his breath as he walked, his ears straining to hear the sound of hoofbeats behind him. A long, slow second passed, and then the wooden floorboards echoed with a hard, rhythmic clickity-clack. Gideon exhaled and glanced behind him. Peanut was following. Sol bellowed and padded after them both. Gideon grinned. Maybe he wasn't so useless after all.

Peanut and Sol followed Gideon all the way back to their pen, trotted inside, and ambled over to the trough for a drink of water after the eventful evening. Gideon shut the gate, latched it, and shook his head. This was not something that happened every day. Or at least, he certainly hoped not.

He turned around to see that the entire family had followed him outside to see what would happen. Naomi raced over to him and grabbed his arm. "You did it!" she said as she bounced onto her toes, then back down again. Gideon grinned. Naomi's enthusiasm was always contagious. It was one of the things that he loved about her. Especially when it contrasted her sisters' serious, reserved nature.

John shook his head. "You're like the Pied Piper." The rest of the family looked at him with a blank expression. John had a habit of mentioning things that the others did not know about, since his parents had left the Amish faith when he was a child. "It's an *Englisch* story about a man who can get anyone to follow him."

Leah laughed. "Even camels?"

"Not sure it mentioned that specifically, but sure." John chuckled. "Gideon just proved it anyway."

"He sure did," Naomi murmured and leaned into Gideon's arm.

An awkward silence fell over the group. Eyes darted from Naomi to Gideon, then to Miriam. A few beats passed.

"Gideon should stay here, with us," Naomi finally said. "He's proven that he has a *gut* heart. He's worked hard ever since he got here. He's respected all of us, including you, Miriam, even when you insulted him."

"I didn't—" Miriam started.

"If you didn't say it outright, then you implied it," Naomi interrupted.

Miriam's mouth tightened into a thin line.

"And it's time I said something." Naomi's chin tilted upward. "To all of you."

Gideon's heart flip-flopped in his chest.

"All of you act as if you know better than me."

"I just want to make sure you're okay," Benjamin said.

Naomi sighed. "I know."

"That's all any of us want," Miriam said.

"I know," Naomi repeated. "But you've got to respect me for who I am. Miriam, you, Amanda, and Leah act as if there's something wrong with me because I believe in love. Especially you, Miriam. And you two—" Naomi pointed to Amanda and Leah "—fell in love, but you didn't want to. You both fought it."

John and David exchanged knowing glances. "That's for certain sure," John said. David chuckled and nodded.

"This family acts as if love is something to avoid," Naomi said. "And all three of you treat me like I'm silly for believing in it."

"We're just more practical," Miriam said.

"*Nee*, you look down on me for it. It's time you accepted me for who I am. I'm a romantic. I love the idea of love. And that doesn't make me shallow or silly or immature."

Miriam sighed. Naomi stared at her, waiting for a response. "You're *recht*," she said after a moment. "I have treated you that way."

"Do you believe in it?"

Miriam hesitated.

"*Vell*, do you?"

"I believe that love makes you vulnerable. You've seen how easily you were fooled in the past."

"But this isn't the past." Naomi squared her shoulders. "This is now. And Gideon isn't any of the other men who tried to court me in the past. He's his own man and deserves to be judged on his own, not lumped together with anyone else."

Gideon could hardly believe it. Naomi was standing up for him in front of her entire family. She was choosing him. And her sisters were listening. Sure, they looked upset, but they weren't falling apart. Gideon's stomach churned with excitement and trepidation. He knew he needed to step in now and defend Naomi. It was time he found his voice too.

Gideon slipped his hand in hers and squeezed. She looked up at him with shining eyes. He could feel the love and trust radiating from her. His heart had never felt so sure or so full. "I love Naomi," he said.

"I knew it!" she said. Then she laughed and shook her head. "I mean, I love you too!" Gideon's attention zeroed in on her for a long, wonderful moment. All that mattered in that moment was her. Not her family, not the farm, not his dreams and disappointments. Only her. She was his dreams, his hopes. As they gazed at one another, he could feel the deep connection, one that did not need words to know it was there. He was doing the right thing and he would not back down.

Gideon tore his attention from Naomi to look directly at Miriam. "I intend to stand by her."

"But you left," Miriam said.

Benjamin took off his straw hat and scratched his head. "And you're headed for Maine, ain't so?"

"Only because I want to prove that I'm worthy of her. I know you all think I'm just after the farm."

Miriam, Amanda, and Leah exchanged quick glances.

"He doesn't need to prove anything—not anymore," Naomi said. "He's already shown us who he is, every day."

Miriam studied Naomi with a tight mouth and unreadable eyes.

Gideon was trying to think of what to say. But Naomi jumped back in with more. "Even the animals can sense that he's got a *gut* heart."

"And the babies," Emma said. "He can always get Caleb to settle down."

Benjamin nodded and put his arm around Emma's shoulder.

"There is something to that," Amanda said. "Animals can sense things."

"That's true," David said.

Miriam put her hands on her hips. "So, you're saying we should trust a camel and a donkey?"

"I like Gideon too," Katie piped up.

The family laughed. David patted Katie's shoulder and smiled. "Katie doesn't take to everyone, you know."

Miriam closed her eyes, took a deep breath, and opened them again. "We don't know you, Gideon. It's nothing personal. We just don't know you."

"I think maybe we do," Benjamin said. He shifted his

weight from one foot to another. "Naomi's got a point. He's not given us any reason to doubt him."

"No red flags, as the *Englisch* say," John said.

"And we've all been looking for them," Leah said.

"Exactly," Naomi said. "And, as hard as you've been looking, you haven't seen any." Naomi narrowed her eyes and stared down Miriam. "If you think you have, tell us right now."

Miriam frowned. She glanced around at the faces waiting for her to answer. "*Nee*. I haven't seen any. Except for what I overheard behind the barn. And it *did* sound like Gideon was after the farm. Plus, you told us that it is his dream to have one. It isn't wrong for us to be cautious."

Gideon felt strange as he watched the exchange, since he was the subject of it. Should he say something? Should he be upset that they had all been watching him for red flags? No, he would have done the same, if he had been in their shoes. He *was* a stranger. People had to be careful because there were bad people out there, with bad intentions. He did not blame them for knowing how the world worked.

But that was not how *he* worked. Some men might use love as a tool to get their way, but he was not one of those men. He never could be one of those men. He could not even understand how it was possible. How could anyone think like that or do something to hurt someone as sweet and trusting as Naomi? It made him angry just thinking about it.

Gideon did not know what he would say before he opened his mouth to speak. But, for the first time in his life, he trusted that the right words would come out. "I love Naomi and I'm standing by her."

Naomi's hand tightened around his.

"I want to..." He realized this was not something to announce to her family. So, he turned his back to them and faced Naomi. Her deep brown eyes filled his heart. They were all he saw. Miriam and the rest of the family faded away. "I never wanted to leave and I'm sorry I did. I don't want to go to Maine. I want to stay here, with you. But only if you want that too. I don't have any money to offer." He frowned as he thought how to explain himself. "But I don't think that's what matters. Not anymore. It would be different if you didn't have a way to support yourself. But I know how much you love Stoneybrook Farm and that you want to keep running it." Gideon stopped and shook his head. He was having a hard time getting to the point. "I want… I mean, I'm hoping…" He swallowed hard. "Naomi, will you marry me?"

Naomi leaped into his arms. "*Ya*! Of course I'll marry you!"

Gideon stumbled back a step, steadied himself, and squeezed her tightly before setting her back onto the ground. He was reeling with emotion. Could this really be happening? The way his pulse was hammering in his throat told him that it must be.

But then he looked up. Naomi's family was staring at him. Everyone was dead silent, except for the sound of Peanut munching on hay in the background. He had been naive to think they would believe him. But he would not let them stop him. He loved Naomi and it would be easy to show them. He was not after money. And he knew how to prove that. "I refuse to take anything from any of you. And I'm going to sign something to show that." He scratched his jaw. There had to be some way to do that. "I'm sure there's some kind of contract that we could make that says I'll never get a share of the farm."

"The *Englisch* do that," John said. "It's called a prenuptial agreement."

"We don't do things the way the *Englisch* do," Leah said. "It doesn't sound *recht*."

"*Ya*, I've never heard of the Amish doing it," John said.

"*Vell*, maybe we have to do things differently," Gideon said. "People have always looked down on me because I don't have any money, even though the Amish aren't supposed to put stock in that kind of thing. But plenty of them do." Gideon shook his head. "I'm going to show you that *I* don't." Gideon felt a surge of strength. He had never spoken out like this before. He had never believed in himself enough. "I have other things—better things—to offer." And, since Naomi said yes to his proposal, those things must be good enough for her. For the first time in his life, he believed it too.

No one spoke for a moment. Gideon's heart thudded in his temples. His stomach churned. But he did not lose his resolve. He knew he was doing the right thing.

"*Nee*." Miriam shook her head.

Gideon's breath caught in his throat. Was she still going to fight him? Was she going to make Naomi choose between them?

"You don't have to sign a contract." Miriam sighed. "I believe you."

"You do?" Gideon did not mean to sound surprised, but he could not help it.

"*Ya*. I do. You've won over the animals and the babies, and now you refuse to take any part of the farm when you marry Naomi." A small smile tugged at Miriam's lips. "I think you've shown us what we needed to see. Naomi's right. It's time we let her make her own choices."

Naomi grinned. "You're only saying that because you know I'm right."

Miriam's smile turned sly. "Do you really think I'd be okay with this if I still thought Gideon was with you for the wrong reasons?"

Naomi rolled her eyes. "*Nee.* And I guess I'm glad to hear it."

The sisters' eyes met and something passed between them. Gideon could sense a shift in the mood and realized that he had just exhaled. How long had he been holding his breath? It felt like for his whole life.

"Besides," Miriam added, "wedding season is months away. There's time for you two to get to know each other better before you tie the knot."

Naomi rolled her eyes. "There's the Miriam I know."

Miriam shrugged and smiled a little wider.

Gideon turned to Naomi. His heart was still beating fast. But now, he knew it was from excitement instead of fear. He had never felt so ready for the future. He had finally found home here, at Stoneybrook Farm, with the woman he loved.

The Stoltzfus family was still staring at him, as if they were waiting for him to stay something. But he had nothing left to say. All that mattered to him was that he was going to marry Naomi. He leaned closer to her and whispered, "So what happens now?"

"We live happily ever after, just like in a romance novel."

"Wait, have you been reading those?" Miriam asked. But her voice was drowned out as everyone else around them erupted into cheers. So, Miriam just shrugged, shook her head, and joined in.

"The end," Gideon whispered to Naomi.

"The end," she whispered back and her face lit up as if she were the happiest woman in the world.

Epilogue

"I want to show you something," Naomi said as she hurried up the long, sloping hill toward the south pasture. Gideon's breath was coming fast as he followed, but Naomi's joy energized him. They had been married yesterday, and each hour felt like a miracle. He thought he might wake up and realize it had all been a dream.

But it was real. It was the marriage that they had been longing for all their lives—even if Gideon had never read a romance novel and had not known how to put that longing into words.

Naomi, on the other hand, had known exactly how a romance should end—or how it should begin, rather. She knew that after the last page of the novel, the love would go on forever. Now, it was up to them to live out that adventure every day, in new and wonderful ways.

"Up there," she shouted as she pointed ahead. The pastureland surrounded them in a green carpet dotted with wildflowers. The air smelled of good, damp earth and clean sunshine. The creek lay just beyond them, sparkling in the bright afternoon light.

Gideon jogged to catch up, then took Naomi's hand as they walked the last few yards together. Naomi turned to look up at him. "See the bridge?"

Gideon's gaze moved to the little footbridge that crossed the stream. The boards had always been a natural wood color. But now they were a cheerful red, just like the little footbridge beside his childhood home. "You remembered," he whispered. Gideon could feel Naomi's eyes on him.

"You like it?" she asked.

Gideon pulled her close, planted a kiss on the top of her *kapp*, and held her. "I love it." He could not believe she had done something so thoughtful. "You painted it yourself?"

Naomi grinned. "Sure did. I wanted you to feel at home, because Stoneybrook Farm is your home now, as much as it's any of ours."

Gideon stood holding her, letting the sunshine warm his face, as his heart overflowed. "I feel it," he said. "And I've felt it since the first time I saw you here. Because wherever you are, home is."

As she snuggled close, Gideon knew that Naomi understood him, and that he understood her. For the first time in his life, he did not feel at a loss for words. Because they did not need words to know that they would always be a home to one another.

* * * * *

Dear Reader,

Welcome back to Stoneybrook Farm! I hope you feel at home here, just as Gideon does. And I hope you had as much fun reading this story as I did writing it. After Naomi's sisters fought against love, I enjoyed creating a free-spirited character who fights *for* it—and shows her family that this fight is worth the risk. You'll have to read the next book in the series to see if Miriam keeps this lesson in mind when her chance for love finally comes....

In the meantime, I would love to stay in touch with you on social media. You can find me at Facebook@VirginiaWiseBooks, Instagram@virginiawisebooks, and virginiawisebooks.com, where you can sign up for my newsletter.

Love Always,
Virginia Wise